The Girl
Next Door

*For Scott Viglietta, Debbie DeSurrey, Mandy Yoder,
and all the young adults taken from us abruptly.*

*For Allie and Holden Caulfield,
for their enduring inspiration.*

*And for Howard Stern, for being there in my
darkest days, leading me to TM, and above all—
reminding me to laugh.*

The Girl
Next Door

Selene Castrovilla

WestSide Books
Lodi, New Jersey

Published by WestSide Books
60 Industrial Road
Lodi, NJ 07644
USA

This is a work of fiction. All characters, places, and events described are imaginary. Any resemblance to real people, places, and events is entirely coincidental.

Library of Congress Cataloging-in-Publication Data

Castrovilla, Selene
  The girl next door / Selene Castrovilla. -- 1st ed.
      p. cm.
  Summary: As seventeen-year-old Sam desperately tries to help her best friend and neighbor Jesse through aggressive treatments for a rare and usually fatal form of cancer, they find themselves falling deeply in love.
  ISBN 978-1-934813-15-7
  [1. Cancer--Fiction. 2. Medical care--Fiction. 3. Sick--Fiction. 4. Best friends--Fiction. 5. Friendship--Fiction. 6. Love--Fiction.] I. Title.
  PZ7.C268746Gir 2010
  [Fic]--dc22

                                                    2010007631

International Standard Book Number: 978-1-934813-15-7
School ISBN: 978-1-934813-40-9

Cover design by Chinedum Chukwu
Interior design by Chinedum Chukwu

Printed in the USA
10 9 8 7 6 5 4 3 2 1

First Edition

The Girl Next Door

Chapter 1

"Life begins perpetually . . .
Life, forever dying to be born afresh,
forever young and eager,
will presently stand upon this earth as upon a footstool,
and stretch out its realm amidst the stars."

—H.G. Wells

Jesse's dying.

The doctors are 96 percent sure of it.

They even have a timeline: seven months. They give him seven months, tops. I try to hold on to hope, but 4 percent is a weak reed to cling to while you're thrashing to keep your head above water.

I caught Jesse crying one morning when he thought I was sleeping. Gwen, his mom, lets me stay over because he's afraid to be alone. He doesn't want to die alone.

I sleep in his old bed; it's on a low iron frame with wheels. Jesse sleeps in his new hospital bed; it's high from the ground, with thick silver bars on the sides and fake wood paneling on the headboard. It's ugly and depressing, but sometimes he's in a lot of pain, and he can move his bed into different positions to get more comfortable.

That morning, I woke to the whirring sound of his bed moving. Then came the slight scrape of metal as he slid the plastic barf tub off the edge of his bedside table and heaved. He throws up a lot from all the chemo crap they put him through.

After, he gargled with the water Maria, the house-keeper, leaves next to the tub every night.

All of a sudden he made this kind of wounded noise and I thought he was gonna heave again, but that wasn't it—he was sobbing.

You can't blame him. One minute he's the star baseball player in high school, class president, and the first junior to be editor of the school newspaper. All down the rows of slamming lockers at Midland Prep you could always hear the name Jesse Parker. Girls wanted to date him. Guys wanted to hang with him to get the excess girls.

The next minute, he's being radiated like Hiroshima, even though the doctors said he was probably gonna die anyway.

They're torturing my best friend.

I cracked my eyes open. The sunshine poured in through his window, right on the wall of shelves with all his trophies and awards facing us. On a beautiful Saturday morning, Jesse should have been buttoning his blue and yellow pinstriped uniform, putting on his cap with the navy "M" over his curly black hair, lacing his cleats, grabbing his bat, and heading into the park. Instead, the uniform and cap hung at the back of his closet, the cleats were tossed who knew where, the bat was leaning in the far corner, and Jess lay in bed, some days barely able to walk.

He probably won't make it to eighteen. He'll never even get to vote.

I didn't know whether I should open my eyes and let him know I was awake—he might get embarrassed. Or maybe he wanted me to wake up.

I opened my eyes.

The first thing I saw was the picture perched on the bedside table next to me. The photo of Jess and his friends at senior movie night last November, back when things were normal, sane. It was in one of those clear Lucite frames, and cracks ran across the middle of the thick plastic, right over the faces. Jess'd smashed it to the floor when I suggested he let his friends come to see him. I didn't bring them up again, but I couldn't just stick them in a drawer, and that's how the photo wound up facing me.

I looked past it and focused on Jess in his bed. He lay with his face in his pillow—not fun for him to do. He told me once that moving after a round of chemo felt like trying to do jumping jacks when you have a stomach virus.

He was crying pretty hard—I could tell by the way his whole body shook, even though the pillow muffled the sound. All I could see of his head was the deep purple skullcap with the peace sign that he insisted on wearing, even though it must have made him too hot. But he didn't need it. I didn't care if he was bald; Gwen certainly didn't care if he was bald; Maria didn't care if he was bald. But he cared. I guess I would, too.

He sucked in his breath, like he was trying to stop sobbing but couldn't. He clenched the pillow, and the bedcovers were pushed down to the knees of his pajamas. He used to sleep in boxers, but he wouldn't wear them with me there, even though I told him it didn't matter. We used to take baths together when we were little, so what difference did it make now?

9

I slid back my thick comforter and stepped on to the cold, bare wood floor. It was only April, but Maria kept the central air turned up on account of Jesse's cap. If I could've opened the window, we'd have gotten a nice fresh breeze; then he wouldn't have needed the a/c. But we'd also have heard the sounds of people playing in Central Park and whiffed the grassy smell.

Jesse never let me open the window.

Goose bumps sprang up across my body as I padded the few feet to him, past the shelves of trophies mounted against the red-striped wallpaper, and past the wheelchair, for bad days, parked beneath them.

"Jess?" I touched the soft cotton shoulder of his pajamas. He flinched.

He lifted his head and looked at me. "Samantha, I'm sorry. . . ."

"Shhh," I said. *What's he sorry for? Waking me up? Crying? Dying?* I stared into his eyes. Even bloodred from crying, they were gorgeous. His irises were hazel, a mix of brown, blue, and green. Stunning.

I climbed over the metal bar—my ankle brushed against it and a chill shot through my leg—and flopped next to him. There was a way to lower the stupid bar, but I could never figure out how. "Mom might not like this," he said, his voice sounding clogged.

"Shhh," I said again. I wiped a tear from his pale cheek. The chemo washed out his color besides knocking him out. He was so weak, I helped him roll on to his back. He winced.

You wouldn't know Jesse was sick by his physique. He'd lost a little weight in the three months since his diagnosis, but he hadn't wasted away.

Jesse's war was internal. The cancer and the chemo were going head-to-head; Jesse's insides were the scorched battlegrounds.

I rested my head against his chest. The fabric of his pajama top was cold, but I could feel the warmth from beneath. Jesse wrapped his arms around me and cried into my long brown hair.

Chapter **2**

"Samantha, your mother wants you home."

The stony voice broke my dream and my eyes popped open. I was in Jesse's arms, and Gwen was shooting me a look that would freeze Hades. I pushed down the covers a little to make it clear I was fully clothed in my purple flannel pajamas.

"Shit," Jesse breathed in my ear. "Hey, Mom," he said to her, way too chipperly. He let go of me, saying, "I guess we slept late. What time is it?"

"Noon." Gwen pushed a stray hair back into place, then folded her arms. "It's noon on a lovely spring day."

"Yeah, whatever." Jesse didn't care about lovely spring days anymore. If it were up to him, we'd be in a permanent winter storm. I think he was still stuck in that snowy January day three months earlier, when this all started.

She sighed and turned to me. "Go home, Samantha."

I avoided her glare, concentrating on the way the sunlight reflected on her glossy red nails. "I was home yesterday."

"I'm sure your mother would like to see you, not just hear the drawers opening, the shower running, and the front door closing behind you." A fat lot she cared what my mother would like, unless it agreed with what she would like—for me to be gone.

"I don't want to go." Even with the a/c, my hair felt as hot on my neck as a wool blanket. I slipped the lavender scrunchy I always slept with from my wrist and wrapped my hair into a ponytail.

"Samantha, I need to speak with Jesse."

I looked at Jess, who'd tugged his skullcap a little further down over his ears, as though he'd like to disappear into it. We both knew he was in for it and he gave my arm a little push. "Go have breakfast, lunch . . . brunch—whatever—with your family. Make 'em happy," he said and pecked my cheek. Gwen's face reddened.

"Okay, fine," I said. I hoisted myself over that stupid railing again, this time banging my shin. "Ow."

"Are you okay?" they both asked. He sincerely, she most likely full of it.

"Yeah." I slunk across the room, grabbed my knapsack with my clothes, and headed for the door. "Later, Jess."

"Later, Sam."

I stepped into the long hallway that connected most of the rooms in the condo—ours had the same layout—and closed his door behind me, but not before I heard Gwen's voice sharpen. "Are you two sleeping together?"

I pressed my ear against the door. "Obviously," he answered, taking the sarcastic approach he'd been using since his diagnosis; it was like he had no time for stupid questions. "You saw us, didn't you?"

"All right, mister smart mouth. Are you having intercourse with Samantha?"

"No."

She went on like he hadn't answered. "Because her mother's had just about enough lately. That'd put her in her grave." Somehow I doubted Gwen stayed up nights agonizing over my mom's health.

"I'd prefer it if you didn't mention graves. I don't really need the visual right now."

"Jesse—" She stopped; he always stopped her cold. She didn't know how to handle him anymore. Jess's dad had walked out on them when Jess was only eight. I couldn't remember what Gwen was like before that because Maria was around way more than she was, but Jess said she used to be nice. But the Gwen I knew was a bitch to Jess, and a complete bitch to me. When she talked to Jess, you could at least spot an occasional chink in her armor, like somewhere under all that steel there was still a beating heart. Before, Jess used to take everything she said; he never talked back, like he was trying to win his mom's approval. But when he got cancer, Jess quit trying.

Gwen sighed. It must have been loud, since I could hear it through the wood. "Jesse, I hope you realize the ramifications that your having sexual relations with Samantha would have on me."

So much for worrying about my mom.

Only Gwen could turn this into something about her. Her son was dying, and she was worried about ramifications; she had the warmth of a reptile. "Do you know the trouble I could be in, allowing her to sleep in this room?" Like the cops were gonna burst in any minute and cuff her or something.

"Mom, for God's sake, Sam's my best friend."

"So you're saying you haven't had sex with her?" He hadn't had sex with anyone, but he sure wasn't gonna share that.

"If we were gonna have sex, wouldn't we have done it years ago?"

"I don't care what you did years ago. I care about what goes on in this room now." So if Jesse had screwed me on my living room sofa when I was fourteen, that was no problem. "I don't want to find her in your bed again. Got it?"

"Okey dokey. Can you take that bucket of barf out for me?"

I could just picture her nose wrinkling. God forbid her designer dress got a splat. "I'll send Maria in for it. She has to bring your breakfast . . . or lunch, I suppose, and your medication."

"Never mind. I'll bring it myself."

"You mean you're eating in the dining room today?"

My eyebrows arched in surprise, hearing that. With the pain he was in, I'd have pegged it a bed day for sure. Then again, in the right mood, Jesse would crawl across the floor inch by inch.

Past the wheelchair.

"Yeah, you'll have to put up with my company for a while. But don't worry, soon you'll have the place to yourself."

15

"Jesse!" Her voice was sharp.

"Hey, it'll even be easier to snag another man. Less baggage."

"Jesse, I . . ." Gwen's voice had lost its edge now. There was a long pause, then she cleared her throat; then there was more silence. Finally she said, "I'm devastated over your situation."

"Yeah, I can see that my *situation* is tearing you apart. But you wouldn't want to ruin your makeup or anything."

Her high heels scuffed against the floor a few times. Quietly she said, "I've done my share of crying, Jesse. What good does it do?"

"None, none at all. See ya in a few, Ma."

Gwen's heels scraped the floorboards some more; I pictured them scuffing back and forth, back and forth. When she spoke again, her voice was back to its usual strength. "We're not done discussing Samantha, Jesse. I told you the rules before I agreed to this insanity."

"Drop it, Ma. I told you, I'm not giving it to Sam."

I wished I could be eighteen—it was only a few months away—and then none of this would matter. Not that we were having sex—but at least maybe then Gwen would leave us alone.

"I only allowed it because of her instability; she looked as though she'd throw herself from the veranda if I said no. Honestly, she's falling apart. I don't know what's going to become of her if—" She stopped, but it was too late. She had the tact of a sledgehammer.

"Not if, Mom, *when* I die," he finished.

There was another long pause. "You're *not* going to die, Jesse. You're not going to die."

"Oh, come on, Mom. We all know what's going to happen. At least *Sam* cares about me."

Her high heels clicked toward me. "I care about you too, Jesse," she said softly and very close to the door—in fact so low, and so far from Jess, that he couldn't have heard her.

I hightailed it into the bathroom a few feet away, twisting the handle as I shut the door so it wouldn't make any noise. I was hiding not only from Gwen, but from the question she'd released into the air; the very same question I'd kept carefully corked in a vial down in the laboratory of my soul. I'd been creaking down those basement steps inside me for weeks, stirring memories in beakers, mixing emotions in test tubes, heating my heart over a Bunsen burner. Trying to concoct some kind of happy ending to answer that question with.

A second later, Gwen clacked down the hall.

I counted to sixty, figuring that gave her enough time to settle in somewhere in the twelve-room condo. I opened the door the same way I closed it—silently—and tiptoed down the hall, past all the twisted-looking modern art paintings Gwen collected—the surreal life.

Halfway, I realized I was still in my pajamas. But I continued moving, even though there was no escape, no way to evade those hovering eight words breathing heat on my neck, raising hairs. They followed me out the door, tapping on my shoulder. They tailed me the few feet along the gold carpet, past the nasty emerald-striped wallpaper the condo association had voted for. I felt like I was in Oz. But where was the wizard when you needed him?

I stood at my door, facing the mauve wreath with halfway-decent fake blue flowers on it. They didn't look hideous, but they sure didn't look real. WELCOME TO THE EVERFIELDS was printed on the wood plaque dangling from it on gold chains. The neighbors hated that thing.

"Go away, go away," I whispered to the words at my back, gripping the doorknob so hard it hurt. But they wouldn't leave.

What will become of me if Jesse dies?

Chapter 3

I'm the girl next door.

I met Jesse the day we moved in, fifteen years ago. People say you don't remember stuff from when you were two, but I do.

Not whole days, but moments.

And feelings.

Even then, it felt like he belonged with me.

My parents had decided that New York City was a better place to raise a child than the hick Long Island town we lived in until Mom hit it big. She writes romance novels—the real schticky kind that everyone claims to hate, but somehow always make *The New York Times* Best Seller List. You should see how the proper ladies in our building frown on Mom's work, but at least some of them had to be reading her books; a million copies of *Moonlight Passion in Paris* didn't get sold to a bunch of men who wanted to read about blossoming crocuses. Anyway, the royalty checks started rolling in, and with them, we rolled into Manhattan—Central Park West.

I don't know what Mom and Dad were thinking. Actually I do, because they told me repeatedly over the years. "Samantha," Mom would say, "New York holds unlimited promise."

Dad would wink and say, "Here, anything can happen."

That's right. Anything can happen. Like your father can snap his briefcase closed, walk you to school, give you a kiss on your forehead and wave goodbye, take the subway downtown, get to work early, and a little before nine o'clock get blindsided by a 747.

But back then, I had no worries, no fears.

From the beginning, from the day my mom wheeled my stroller across the white and gold marble floor in the lobby and into the shiny black elevator, I had Jess.

The elevator climbed, lifting us to our new home. Ding! The doors slid open and another stroller faced me. In it sat a chubby-faced, wide-eyed boy with bushy black hair. His cheeks spread even wider in a huge smile. He laughed and clapped, and I leaned forward as far as I could, reaching for him. . . .

I took a breath, let it out slowly, and turned the knob.

"Sam!" Teddy, my five-year-old, cherub-faced brother, clomped down the hallway toward me. His feet were about a third the size of his shoes—Mom's black pumps, the ones she wears at book signings. Her pearls—also for signings—shifted back and forth across the collie picture on his shirt, and her diamond brooch—a gift from Dad she never wore—was pinned against the shirt dog's alert ear.

I bent down and grabbed him up tight.

"Sam, Sam, can you play house with me?" he begged. His big, round, green eyes pleaded. Poor Teddy, he missed me.

I patted his sandy hair. "Ted, I'm sorry, I just don't feel like playing right now." I couldn't do it. I didn't have it in me.

"What about Jesse?" His eyes flickered, still hopeful. "Can he take me to play catch?" Jesse used to do that all the time. He loved Teddy as much as I did.

"No, Ted, he can't." God, I would have given anything if he could. Anything.

"Oh, fine." With a final, sad look, Teddy gave up and clomped off to his room.

"Baby, you're home!" Mom came from the kitchen, apron draped over her usual sweats, and hugged me tight. "Are you having lunch with us?"

"Yeah, Mom." I tried to smile for her, but it didn't happen.

"Fantastic!" Her face lit up like a Roman candle.

Teddy was back, tugging at my pajama sleeve. "Sam, Sam, do you want some tea?" He was holding his little china teapot in his other hand.

"Sure, Ted."

About a year ago, Mrs. Pinchon, our blue-haired, prune-faced neighbor in the left corner apartment, made a comment in the elevator to Mom about Teddy dressing up in Mom's clothes. Mom let her have it, in her calm "mom" way. She said that our society allowed girls to be tomboys or just about anything they wanted, while boys were crated up in little masculine boxes. She said she didn't know or care if Ted's style meant that he was gay. What mattered was that he was a free spirit, and she wasn't going to clip his wings.

"I finally have a daughter," Mom said, pointing to Teddy's getup as he pranced off to get a teacup. It was true; I wasn't much of a girl. Never a dress, not one dab of makeup, and not even a clip in my hair. Getting fancy takes way too long.

Mom was no fashion queen either, in her sweats, which she used to wear for an average of three days a week and now wore a solid seven since Dad died two and a half years ago. She kept her ginger hair ultrashort so she didn't have to do anything with it in the morning, and she only wore lipstick to public appearances.

"Enjoy her," I said. We laughed together. That felt real good.

I went to my room to get dressed. I used to love it in there; a few years ago Mom found me the coolest vintage iron bed in Greenwich Village. Weathered white, with swirling curves all around, the metal looked like it was dancing. My bedspread was a bohemian plum and white patchwork quilt. It practically called you to come lie on it.

The rest of the room was just as relaxing. There were sheer lavender curtains over the windows, a purple peacock chair sat in the corner, and a turquoise beanbag chair rested across from it next to a floor lamp topped by a pastel-beaded shade.

My shadowbox desk displayed a bunch of snapshots under its glass top. Most were of Jesse and me. In the tub at three and four, going down the gigantic Central Park slide at ages eight and nine, in the sand at Jones Beach at twelve and thirteen, at the Broadway show *Mamma Mia* last year. We'd had so much fun, we'd bought an Abba album the next day.

I needed to get through lunch. Just get through lunch, and then back to him . . .

I grabbed some jeans and an old blue T-shirt that said SO WHAT? from my dresser, the top of which was crammed with memorabilia ranging from a purple kitten to a tall glass jar of seashells, and got dressed. I pulled yesterday's clothes from my knapsack and packed in a clean pair of pajamas.

I hit the light switch on my way out and closed the door behind me.

"So how's Jesse feeling?" Mom asked, handing me the cole slaw she'd made from scratch.

"He had a bad night, but he's better now."

"Is Jesse still sick?" Teddy asked. He now wore Mom's pink hat with the feather attached, which I for one thought looked better on him anyway.

"Yes, honey, he's still sick," Mom said.

"When's he gonna get better?"

I couldn't answer; I couldn't even look at him.

"I'm not sure, honey," said Mom. We didn't know how to break it to Ted, so we never did.

Teddy took a big bite of his chicken cutlet. "Can I go see him?" he asked, with a chunk of chicken hanging out of the side of his mouth.

"Don't talk with your mouth full, honey," said Mom.

"Yeah, okay," I said. Jesse would like to see him, too. "You can come with me after lunch."

"Samantha, can't you stay a while longer?" Mom's question wasn't demanding, wasn't harsh; it just was.

"Mom, I—" I realized my mouth was full; I gulped, feeling the lump slide down my throat. "I need to—"

"All right, baby," she interrupted. "Let's just chat a little and finish up. Then you can go back."

Chapter 4

"Hey, sporto!" Jesse broke into a big smile when Teddy dashed into his room ahead of me. He lowered the bar on his bed and held out this arms. "C'mere."

Teddy leaped onto the bed like a frantic terrier and threw himself on Jesse. "Take it easy, Teddy," I said.

"It's okay, I feel okay now," Jesse said. Teddy grabbed a pillow and whacked him in the face with it.

"Teddy!" I scolded, sounding like a mother, for sure.

"Sam, chill. It's fine," Jess said. I knew he felt bad for not giving Teddy the attention he was used to. "Sorry we can't take off, buddy," he told Teddy. Jesse always gave Teddy rocket ship rides. He'd launch Teddy and fly him all around the room—the whole apartment—in his arms, on a space adventure to Mars.

"That's all right," Teddy said, trying to climb on Jesse's head. Good thing he'd taken off the pumps. "We can do it when you get better."

Jesse stared out from between Teddy's legs. "Yeah, bud. Okay."

25

I bit my lip to keep from bursting into tears, whether for Jess, or Teddy, or me, I couldn't say.

Free of the metal bar, I sank onto the corner of his bed. "Hey, how was lunch with mama?"

Teddy tugged at Jesse's hat. "Whoa, sporto. I need that." He looked at me. "How'd you know I had lunch with my mother?"

"I listened at the door."

"Ahhh." He lifted Teddy's shirt and tickled, making him cackle. "It sucked. I only did it to pi—" He stopped, realizing Teddy was listening. "I only did it to annoy her, really."

"Jesse, why do you always wear a hat?" Teddy asked.

"Teddy, stop asking questions," I snapped.

"But why does he wear a hat in his room?"

I couldn't deal with questions; it was enough just walking around. "Say goodbye to Jesse." I stood and reached for Teddy. "It's time to go."

He wrapped his arms around Jesse's shoulders. "Nooo," he wailed. "I just got here."

I tugged at his hands to release them from Jess. "It's time to *go*," I repeated. But I couldn't pry him loose.

"That's enough," said Jesse, giving me a little push. He looked hard at Teddy, scrunching his eyebrows. "Listen, sporto. Can you handle a grown-up kind of conversation?"

Teddy nodded.

"Even if it's really sad?"

Teddy nodded, slowly this time.

"Sit right here next to me," Jesse said, thumping on the mattress. Teddy plopped down.

Jesse put his arm around Teddy's shoulders. "I wear this hat because of my disease."

Teddy blinked at him. "Are you cold?"

"No. It's because the treatment they're doing made me lose my hair."

"What?" exclaimed Teddy. "Can I see?"

Jesse swiped off his skullcap; he was as bald as Mr. Clean.

"Cool! Can I touch your head?"

Jesse bent for Teddy to reach. Teddy smoothed his hand around and around, like his fingers were skating on Jesse's head.

When he stopped, Jesse said, "Okay, now here's the sad part. Ready?"

Teddy nodded.

"The disease that I have . . . there's no way to cure it. The doctors don't know how."

Teddy frowned. "But you said they're doing something. . . ."

"They're treating me, but it's not enough."

Teddy's face filled with confusion. "What does that mean?"

Jesse took in a breath. He gave me a questioning look. I nodded to go ahead, even though a big piece of me wanted to stop him. "It means, sporto, that I'm going to heaven in a few months."

No, no, I thought. *Fight it, Jess. Fight it.*

Teddy's eyes bulged. "Heaven?"

"Yeah." Jesse squeezed into Teddy's arm.

27

"Will you . . ." Teddy hesitated, then blurted, "Will you tell my daddy I said hi?"

"Yeah. I'll do that, sporto," Jesse said. A tear ran down his cheek. "I'll do that."

It turned out that Teddy handled the news better than anyone, especially me. In the emergency room, when the doctor told us about the tumor, I'd gotten so hysterical that they wanted to give me a shot. But I calmed myself down. Otherwise, they wouldn't have let me see Jesse.

Earlier in the evening, he'd starred in *Romeo and Juliet* in the school play, opposite Cindy Evans. She was his most frequent girlfriend, not that I got why. Sure, she was gorgeous, perfection from her auburn-highlighted hair to her cherry red polished toenails. She reminded me of Barbie—complete with plastic personality. I'd never understood how Jesse could stand being around her, except I guess they didn't talk much. They were heavily into public spit-swapping, never failing to nauseate me at the lunch table. They'd broken up yet again about a month earlier, but apparently crooning Shakespeare to her perfectly made-up features made him miss sucking face because he'd told me he was planning on asking her out again at the cast party that night—closing night.

The play went smoothly, until the end. When Jess drank that poison and collapsed, he gave the most convincing cry I'd ever heard.

Convincing, because it was real.

Jesse didn't get up for his bow. He couldn't—he was in agony.

A sharp pain was shooting down his arm, like a knife stabbing him.

He'd kept quiet until Juliet "died," not wanting to ruin the show.

Hours later, a doctor who looked about my age explained to Gwen, Maria, my mom, and me that a tumor was in Jesse's spine. I let out a cry even louder than Jesse's from the stage.

Two days later, I sat in the thick-cushioned chair next to Jesse during visiting hours. We were craning our necks to watch *Law and Order* on the TV mounted to the wall, trying not to think about real life. Hard to do, when there was an IV needle stuck in Jesse's vein, flooding him with painkillers. He'd been zoning in and out, but they weren't enough to numb the fear.

The room looked like a botanical garden. The school, the baseball team, all of his friends' families, and more had sent bouquets of good wishes. He got about a year's worth of metaphors and similes for my mom, but the too-sweet smell of the flowers made my nose itch.

At the commercial, Jesse asked again if I wanted some of the mixed vegetables, apple cobbler, meat that looked like greyish turkey, or wheat bread that sat untouched on the swivel tray in front of him. Appetizing as it was, I couldn't eat, either.

The door pushed open. Another doctor, older this time,

liver spotted and wrinkled, walked in. He was wearing a striped tie, a stethoscope, and a no-nonsense expression.

Jesse reached his hand over the bed rail and I took it in mine. His whole arm was trembling.

After a curt greeting he might have saved for all the good it did, the doctor opened his steel chart-holder and brushed through some pages.

Without any further ado, he told Jesse that he had non-Hodgkin's lymphoma. But not just any kind; his was called small noncleaved, non-Burkitt's lymphoma. And, he had a really special thing called a c-myc translocation. That, apparently, was the kicker. A death sentence, delivered with the same emotion as a waiter mechanically reciting the blackboard specials.

Except Jesse's menu had no choices.

He'll have the cancer, medium well.

Jesse got so depressed, he barely spoke for the rest of the two weeks he spent in the hospital. I kept telling him it wasn't hopeless. People survive cancer a lot these days.

But not when they had small noncleaved, non-Burkitt's lymphoma with a dual translocation of c-myc and bcl-2, which I really didn't understand at all. Whatever that dual translocation was, it changed the survival rate from about 80 percent to zero.

I went online at home and looked up the disease. I read studies. According to them, no one with a dual translocation of c-myc and bcl-2 had lived more than ten months. Ten months was fantastic, actually. Woo-hoo.

The only good thing—if anything about this could be called good—was that because Jesse's cancer was considered the most aggressive lymphoma, they were researching it intensively, combining new drugs and different levels of radiation, and trying experimental treatments. They were hopeful that patients would begin to live longer.

That's what they based Jesse's 4 percent chance on—that they'd get lucky with him. Even though they'd never gotten lucky with anyone else.

Jesse insisted I show him all my research; that was pretty much the last conversation I had with him while he was in the hospital. I tried to convince him that he could be the one—he could be the first survivor. He didn't say anything in response. He just shut down.

I noticed a sign about "the Stroke Club" meetings by the elevator as I was leaving one night. That got me thinking—there had to be support groups for people with cancer, too. I went back online and found a whole bunch of chat groups Jess could join, and even some in-person groups in New York City. But Jess didn't so much as blink when I told him the next day, and all the information I'd printed out about them sat untouched on his bedside table.

A parade of doctors spoke to Jesse and Gwen. She was no help, no support. She turned Jesse's tragedy into the hysterical Gwen show, sobbing into the tissues offered by sympathetic, eligible doctors. The hospital became her personal pick-up joint. There was really something wrong with that woman.

Maria sat with Jesse a lot during the days, when I was in school. She probably spent most of the time mouthing silent prayers. I love Maria, but she's into this religion called Santeria, which seems like voodoo to me. She brought a thick red candle in a glass jar that was supposed to ward off bad spirits, but she wasn't allowed to burn it in the hospital. Undeterred, she brought her aerosol spray can of Go Away, Evil! (which conveniently doubled as an air freshener) and *ppsshh'd* it liberally into the air until Jess had a coughing fit so loud that a nurse came hurrying in.

Now there was a chicken's foot inside Jess's bedside drawer (even in his darkest mood he'd humored Maria, wordlessly accepting the foot, then chucking it out of sight) to drive away the demons or whatever it was she thought was hurting Jesse. She couldn't consider the possibility that the cancer cells had formed in some biological way.

I guess it's no different from the way some people pray to Jesus, with their statues, holy water, and rosary beads. It's hard for me to wrap my mind around any of these rituals, having been raised with none. My mom always says she's spiritual but not religious. She's big into karma, and thinks being a good person and doing the right thing are what count. The problem with karma is that it's so abstract. There're no props. Sometimes I want something more to hold on to. But a leap into faith seems way too wide.

Jess was used to Maria's ways; his mom didn't give him any religion either, so Santeria was all he had. When we were little, we'd watch Maria doing her incantations like she was performing a magic show. As he got older, Jess didn't buy into Maria's rituals actually working, but he liked that she thought they would.

At least, he used to. Who knew what he felt now?

He told me once that he wished he could believe in something, too. That was a long time ago. Now I wished it, too. I wished it so badly—for us both, but especially for him.

Maria brought Jess stuff from home. His toothbrush. His iPod—which sat untouched, as far as I saw. And his pajamas. He could only wear the bottoms. He needed to be in the hospital gown because of the IV, and because they were constantly doing crap to him. Sticking him with needles. Sticking him under or into machines. More tests, plus combination chemotherapy and radiation. He was red enough to be served on a plate with melted butter.

And by the end of the two weeks, hairs were falling all over his gown.

My mom visited him a lot, too, when Teddy was at preschool. She's good at comforting and pep talks—she probably could have been one of those motivational speakers who show you how to change your life, or a spiritual advisor, or something—but Jesse wasn't open to anything. She told me he didn't speak to her either, or even look at her. She told me not to take it personally, that he did that to me. He was in shock, numb. Eventually he'd come back to me.

She told me the only thing I could do was be there for him.

I was actually the only friend Jess put up with. Pete, Jess's best friend after me, came by one day. At first things went okay—as okay as things with Jesse went. Pete said how everyone missed Jess, how nothing was the same without him. Jesse pretty much grunted his contributions to the conversation. Then Pete opened up the shopping bag he'd brought with him and took out a baseball mitt. He held it up, showed Jess all the writing on it. "The team signed this for you, instead of a card," he said. He tried handing it to Jess, but Jess just stared at him. Then Jess raised his fist and punched at the plates on his swivel tray, sending them crashing to the floor.

Lumpy greyish egg salad, splat.

Lumpy greyish soup, splat.

Red gelatin bounced from its foam container, then broke apart, rupturing into glistening crimson shards and spotting the rest of the sallow mess, some of it hitting Pete. And Pete just stood there, a smorgasbord of splotches, blinking and holding that glove. He didn't get why Jesse was so angry at him.

But Jesse wasn't mad at Pete; Pete just represented all the things that Jesse was missing.

It would've been great if Jess had at least spoken. Screamed something, even. But he didn't. Pete mumbled an apology for upsetting Jess and backed out of the room. Even though he wasn't my favorite person, I felt bad for him. After that, none of Jess's other friends were even allowed upstairs in the hospital.

Every afternoon I sat in that room with Jess, from four o'clock until a little after eight, when they threw me out. On weekends I was there from ten on. Every day I tried and tried to get through a brick wall. Inside, I felt the panic rising. A nightmare—it had to be a nightmare.

But it wasn't.

Jesse stared at the specks in the foam white ceiling while I did frenzied, internal flips. *How can he give up? Jesse always wins. He succeeds at everything he tries.*

He just has to fight.

He can beat this.

We can beat this.

If he would just come back and fight.

When Jess was released, when he came home to his new hospital bed, he finally started speaking to me again. But he was different. Distant. Lost.

He was nice to me, at least. Not sarcastic like he got with Gwen. He wanted me to stay with him. I needed to stay with him. But he made it clear he didn't want to talk about hope. He wanted me to zip up, not say a word on the subject. Then he settled into the muck of submission, burying himself in the mud.

And I cried myself to sleep every night.

Chapter 5

"Hey Samantha, you awake?"

"Kind of." I'd been dozing off into a hazy sleep.

Jess's voice came out of the dark, like from nowhere. "Do you believe in heaven?"

I propped myself up with my elbows and thought. It was a hard question; I didn't believe in pearly gates and a guy with a beard. *But there has to be something. Doesn't there?*

"I guess."

"Don't guess. Yes or no."

"Yes." Like I'd say no, anyway.

"Aww, you wouldn't say no, anyway."

I reached for the lamp and clicked it on. My elbow brushed the picture frame next to it, and I glanced at the distorted people behind fractured plastic. "Why'd you ask then?"

He was facing the wall. "I don't know . . . just to make conversation."

"Can't sleep?"

"Not so much."

"How 'bout you turn around?"

He didn't answer.

"Jess?"

Nothing again.

I flipped the covers off and went over to his side of the room. "I refuse to speak to your back."

He moved on to his back, slowly. His face was red and blotchy.

I touched his cheek, rubbing away moisture. "Jess, it's okay to cry."

"Two nights in a row. You must think . . ."

In world history we'd learned about cups the ancient Hebrews used to save their tears. The fuller the tear cup, the higher the person was esteemed. I'd have to remind Jess about the sacramental tears when he was up for a conversation.

For now I said, "I think you need a friend."

I leaned over the bar and took him in my arms. *My best friend.*

My best friend.

"Time to wake up, my young friends."

I heard the swoosh of the curtains parting and felt the sun shine on me, even with my eyes shut. I opened them and Maria was swiping Jesse's trophies with a green feather duster.

"I need to clean dis room," she said in her Spanish accent. "It is sty."

Not that I could see, but then again, Maria had high standards.

As usual, Maria was immaculate. Her charcoal hair was pulled back and piled into a bun, with not a hair out of place. Her grey uniform was crisp and spotless.

"Maria," Jesse said, "I've been meaning to ask you to take those trophies away. Can you stick them in the closet or something?"

"Why you wanna do that? You gotta be proud!"

"Must you argue about everything?" he asked with a groan.

But he was only kidding. Maria was more of a mom to him than Gwen. She'd always taken care of him. She'd given us our baths, and it was she who'd pushed the stroller the day I met Jess.

"Yes, I do gotta argue about ev'ythin'," she said, hands on her hips. "And why doncha get outta dis bed and go outside?" She gave him a poke with the feather duster.

"I got out of bed yesterday." He folded his arms. *Stubborn, I tell you.*

"Today's not yesaday." True enough. "You gonna get out by youself or am I gonna make you get out?" She poised her duster threateningly.

"Okay, okay." He pushed back his sheets, lowered his bar, and slowly swung his legs down. "Ow," he winced.

I jumped up. "You need help, Jess?"

"Let 'im try by hisself, Sammy. It's betta dat way." She gave me a wink and turned to him. "Unless you wan' da wheelchair?"

"No chair." He hated that thing. And Gwen had to park it right in front of him. Bitch.

"You go for walk wit' Sammy."

"C'mon, Maria. I can't."

"You gonna go for walk, or she pushes you," Maria said, pointing at him with the duster. "Wheech one?"

"I'll walk." He rolled his eyes.

"Dat's betta. I go getch you medicine, den you two eat nice breakfast, den you walk." She strode to the door, still brandishing her duster. She gave it one final jab toward Jesse. "And don' let me fin' out you sat in da lobby or anytin' like dat."

"Sam," he started the minute she left.

"Don't ask me to lie for you," I warned, pointing my finger. "You gonna go for walk."

His mouth crinkled into a smile.

Jesse could walk, at least on good days. It was just that he looked kind of bizarre doing it; he'd lost some of his muscle control and couldn't coordinate his movements. His body veered.

We were outside maybe five minutes when he swung his arm around my shoulder for support. He couldn't stand it—not being in command of his own body.

He didn't say anything, and neither did I. We just hobbled along the sidewalk next to the park. A typical Sunday in New York City. Loud. Horns honking, radios blasting, people yakking on their cells as they hurried to who knew where. There're no days of rest in New York City. There's just hectic and frenzied; that's it.

Inside the park it would have been quieter, but Jess never wanted to go in there; I didn't even ask. Jesse didn't want to be around the people in the park—playing, lounging, or whatever they were doing. They reminded him of what he was losing.

But more than that, the park itself represented what Jesse was losing. He'd grown up there. From the swings to the ball field, the park was Jesse's life. And he'd turned his back on life, on hope. It was easier for him to avoid it. Acceptance was his pain pill.

But it wasn't a pill I could swallow.

We moved slowly, probably looking like lovers. He in denim, me in a Windbreaker. Finally we sat on a bench. Jesse hadn't eaten much of his French toast—he'd just shoved it around his plate; so I got us a couple of hot dogs from a cart and we sat on a bench outside the park wall. Jess stared at the food in his hand.

"So about that heaven thing," he said. "Do you think we go somewhere, or is this the end of the road?"

It was so hard to talk about this, especially in the harsh daylight, without the veil of shadows.

"I think we go somewhere," I said. "I just don't know where. Maybe we come back, like in that movie *Dead Again*." We'd watched it about a year ago, with my mom. It's about a husband accused of killing his wife, then being executed for it. They're both reincarnated, find each other again, and uncover the truth behind the murder.

He shifted, creaking the wooden bench; we were silent for a while, watching traffic go by. I was more than halfway done with my hot dog, but he hadn't even started on his.

"Will you keep my ashes?" he asked.

"Huh?" I almost choked midchew. *What a question.*

Jesse sucked some sauerkraut off the top of his hot dog and asked again. "Will you keep my ashes?"

I swallowed the rest of my bite. "I didn't even know you wanted to be cremated," I said softly. I set the rest of my food down on the edge of the bench.

"I just decided." He chewed a bite and swallowed. "I don't like the idea of worms and stuff crawling all through me."

I felt a chill and zippered my jacket.

"Well?"

I looked at him blankly. He had ketchup on his lip. I wiped it and then licked my finger clean.

"Hello? Are you gonna answer me?"

I didn't want to picture Jesse in a jar. "Yeah," I said. "Of course—if Gwen lets me."

"I'm gonna make a will. I'm gonna leave my ashes to you."

I patted his leg. "Jess, you're only seventeen. I don't think it'll be legal."

He gave me an intense look. "Then I'll have to make it to eighteen." He stuffed the rest of his hot dog into his mouth. When he finished chewing he put his arm around me. "'Cause I'm not sitting on Mom's mantle while she serves coffee and cake to her dates."

We sat silently on the bench for a while, listening to the sounds of the city and breathing in its scents while our food settled into our stomachs. Two boys in green and yellow baseball uniforms passed us, springing down the sidewalk in front of their chatting moms. The boys looked a little older than Teddy. One of them vaulted to the sidewalk corner and called to the other to catch. He arced his arm back to pitch, causing several nearby pedestrians to halt, ready to duck. Both mothers broke in, chirping out a simultaneous, *"No!"*

"Don't let Mom chuck my stuff, okay?" Jess said softly, slipping his fingers into mine. I guessed the boys made him think of his baseball days, and his gear.

"Gwen wouldn't throw your trophies out."

"I'm not talking about just them. I'm talking about all my . . . *stuff*—" He stumbled on that last word. He was quiet for a moment, then said, "Everything in my room."

Thinking of Jess's room without Jess in it sucked. I didn't say anything, just squeezed my fingers into his. He didn't need me to answer; he just needed me to listen.

"That's all that's gonna be left of me, Sam." His voice was barely there. It was soft and light, a feather disappearing with the wind.

"Oh, Jess," I said, pulling him tight against me. His heart was beating so hard through that denim. "That's not true."

"It . . . is . . ." He was speaking through phlegm.

My fingers smoothed over his shoulder blades and back, skimming over rough, thick fabric as my mind worked. I knew what I wanted to say, but I wasn't sure how to say it. "Your things don't make you, Jess," I whispered into his ear. "All the stuff in your room, it doesn't add up to you. It's only . . . stuff."

"So . . . I'll just be . . . gone?"

"No, no." I pressed my hand into his back, willing strength into him. "Whether there's reincarnation or not, you'll be here. You'll be with me, in my heart. As long as I live, so will you."

I held him for a while. Finally he pulled back and looked into my eyes. I know it was an effort for him to do it because his eyes were so, so scared. "Do you . . . really believe that?" he asked, his voice quavering still.

I stared back without blinking. "I do."

"How was school today?" Mom asked on Monday afternoon. I was heading into my room to do my homework. That was the deal. Homework at home, and then I could leave.

"Fine."

"You sure about that?" Mom looked pissed; very un-Mom-like.

"Yeah. Why?"

"You sure you were in school today?"

Shit. "How'd you find out?"

"The school called. You've been absent quite a bit, it seems." She crossed her arms. "I'm waiting for an explanation here, Samantha."

I threw my knapsack down and fell back against the wall. "I meet Jesse at the hospital when he gets his treatments. Gwen never goes with him; he needs me, Mom."

Mom still looked pissed. "I know that, Sam, but you need to think about your future. You can't skip school and still pass. What's going to happen to you?"

"I'll get by."

"You're not getting by! Mr. Hensley said you're failing math and English. English!" That really pissed her off, her being a writer and all, even if it was ultra corny writing. Her arms waved in my face. "He said if you don't go to summer school, you'll be left back."

"Then I'll be left back."

"You went from being an honors student in tenth grade to flunking the eleventh grade. You're destroying your life!" Tears streamed down her face. I hated giving her more crap; I really did.

"Mom, take it easy." It was so weird, this whole scene. It felt like there was a barrier between us—an invisible wall. "It'll all work out. I'll fix my life someday. I promise."

Her face was streaked and she sniffled, all stuffed up. I fingered through my pocket and pulled out a crumpled tissue for her nose.

She made a trumpeting sound when she blew. It would've been funny some other time. "Will you?" she asked.

"Huh?"

"Will you fix your life?"

"Eventually."

Chapter 6

There was this whole other problem, on top of everything else.

Jesse didn't want to die a virgin. He never came out and said it, but I knew.

He'd done some stuff with lots of girls, but he'd never done *that*. I think it was my fault; I told him it wasn't right to take a girl's virginity if he didn't love her. I'd asked him what he'd think if some guy did that to me? So, now that I'd blown his chances, I had to do something about it.

I thought about getting him a hooker, but where would I get one? From down on Tenth Avenue? I didn't want to go down there alone, and I heard most of them were guys anyway. Poor Jess. Imagine if I brought him a guy by accident!

I could call an escort service from the ads in *The Village Voice*. I heard some of them were hookers. But which ones? And would a hooker come if we were minors? What if Gwen came home while she was there? And what if the hooker gave him some disease? I mean, he's dying and all, but suppose they came up with a cure for his cancer, but she gave him AIDS? I heard you could get it even with a condom sometimes.

In the end, I realized it was much easier and safer to just do it myself, give myself to him.

He didn't ask me; it was my idea. And it surprised the heck out of him.

It was the middle of the night when I climbed into his bed. I'd woken up, and something told me it was the right time. He hadn't had chemo for two weeks, so he'd been feeling stronger. He'd had a really good few days; he'd walked outside with me again, and he hadn't barfed at all.

The room was pitch black, and on the way over I tripped on the wheelchair; he didn't wake up, though. I unbuttoned my pajamas, slipped them off, and hoisted myself over the rail. I gasped when my butt touched the metal, but he still didn't wake up. The room was the temperature of a meat locker, and goose bumps ran up my arms and legs. I shoved myself under the covers and shook him.

"Jess?"

"Huh?" he grunted.

"Jess, wake up."

He squinted at me through one eye. "What? Why are you in my bed?"

"I want to give you something."

"What do you want to give me, at this hour"—he turned his head and looked at the glowing red numbers on his alarm clock—"one fifty-two in the goddamn morning?"

I lowered the comforter; he sucked in a breath of shock. "Have you lost your mind?"

"It's okay. We love each other, don't we?"

"Not that way. And you're like, my little sister, for God's sake."

"I'm two weeks older than you," I said. It was true; we were both born in December. I was a grade behind because my parents started me in school a year later than his had.

He smiled—he couldn't help it. "Well, you're still like my sister."

"I'm not your sister," I said, touching him. "I'm just the girl next door."

He removed my hand. "I can't move around like I used to. . . ."

I kissed his lips. "I'll do the moving for you."

He gave me a little shove. "Sam, I can't do this."

"I told you, it's okay. I want you to."

"No, I mean I *really* can't do this."

I touched him again. "I beg to differ."

He traced his fingers across my arm, pushing the hairs back down. "You're freezing. Put your top back on."

"I'll be okay. I want you to have the full effect." I reached over and turned on his lamp.

He laughed. It was so great to hear him laugh.

Sitting there all exposed was pretty freaky, though. I felt so vulnerable, so—naked. I was glad it was Jess; I don't think it could have been anyone else.

I sat on his lap. He moved himself forward. I touched his sweet face. Perfect, except for one thing. "Do me a favor? Lose the hat."

He pulled it off and threw it to the floor. Bald or not, he was damn good-looking. "You're beautiful, Jess," I told him. "I love you."

"I love you, too, Samantha."

We kissed, probing. It felt weird, but in a good way. I'd never even done it before, but I'd read up on it in my mom's books. I grabbed a condom I'd put on the night-stand. I'd bought three at the corner store the week before—they have them in bins next to the lollipops at the counter—three for four dollars. The wrapper crinkled in my hands as I fumbled, ripping it open. And there it was in my palm—a flimsy elastic disc.

He studied me with his big, gorgeous eyes. "Sam, are you sure?"

"I'm sure."

It was over pretty fast. The red numbers on his clock said 2:12 a.m. Wow, was he grateful. He kept kissing me, and babbling that it was better than he'd ever dreamed it could be. He was happy for the first time since he found out he had cancer. I felt glad for him, but I didn't really enjoy it. It hurt—like something scraped through me—a chisel, maybe.

He smiled and kissed me for like the ten billionth time. "Hey, did you like it?"

I wanted to lie, but I couldn't; I gave him this vague nod. He knew.

"Sam, I'm sorry. . . ."

"It doesn't matter."

"It does."

"This was for you, not me."

"It was your first time, too. I ruined it." He looked crushed.

"There's plenty of time for me to learn how," I said. It was the wrong thing to say; he just stared at the trophies on the wall.

"Jess, I didn't mean it that way. I just meant—Jess, look at me." I grabbed his face and turned it toward me. Now my hot tears fell. "I wanted to do this for you, not me. I wasn't even thinking about me."

He wiped my tears. "Great, now you're crying. I'm something, aren't I? A real selfish prick."

"No, you're not. . . ." I tried to stop crying, but I couldn't.

"C'mere."

"Why?"

"Just c'mere."

I sniffed and swiped at my face. "What?"

He started touching me. "I should have done this before. I wasn't thinking straight. You woke me up and shocked me and all."

"Forget it. You don't have to—"

"Will you quit talking and enjoy yourself?"

"I—I—" Suddenly I couldn't form a sentence; words didn't matter. Prickly warmth erupted inside, and I was experiencing things I never would have believed.

I felt my crocus blossoming.

"How was that?" he asked.

I still couldn't speak. My head was spinning; I felt like I was floating. "Good," I finally managed.

His hand was on my thigh, warm and loving. "Listen," he said, squeezing a little. "You got another condom?"

Chapter 7

We made love whenever he could. He was a different person in bed—happy. And I was happy, too. I just made sure to go back into my bed afterward. One mess-up and Gwen would throw me out.

Maria knew. She cornered me in the kitchen after school one day. I was making ham sandwiches for Jess and me.

"Sammy." She touched my arm as I shredded lettuce.

"Yeah?" I kept cutting.

"Jesse, hees in betta mood lately."

"Yeah?" I sliced up a tomato.

"And you . . . you have dis glow. . . ."

I looked up. "A glow? I don't think so." I went back to my project, rolling up slices of ham and placing them on the bread.

Her hand gripped my shoulder. "Sammy, I jus' wan' you ta be careful."

I closed the sandwiches up. "Careful?"

"Sammy, hee's dyin'. . . ."

I whipped around sharply, looking her in the face.

"Dying? He's dying? Why do you say that? How can you say *that*?" The words poured out, burning hot. "Don't you believe in your spells and chanting anymore? Can't the spirits save Jess—" As suddenly as I'd begun my rant, I stopped. I could barely get Jess's name out—it was like I'd choked on it.

"Sammy." Maria had both hands on my shoulders now. "Sammy, we all doin' what we can, but you gotta face da facts."

"The facts can go to hell," I said, so maturely. "With all that doctors can do, why can't they save him? Why can't *someone* save him?" It wasn't like my dad, gone without warning. Jess was here, he was still here, he had a chance. . . .

"I don' know, Sammy. . . . They tryin', we all tryin' our best for him. But what about you?" We stayed like that for a long minute. I felt her stare, but I kept my focus on the sandwiches waiting for me on the counter. Jess was waiting for me, too. I just wanted to go back and be with him. Was that so much to ask?

She let go of my shoulders. "You gotta protect youself. You gettin' deeper—too deep."

Still looking away, I picked up my plates. "I'll be okay." I brushed against her apron as I left.

"I hope so, Sammy," I heard behind me. "I hope so."

Jesse threw up the sandwich. "I'm sorry," he said between heaves. "I liked . . . *bluuh* . . . it. Really . . . *bluuh* . . ."

I didn't care about the sandwich and I told him so. He rinsed out his mouth, then pulled himself up, lurching painfully into the bathroom to gargle.

Poor Jess, back on his chemo cycle. Just when he was getting used to not barfing.

I got rid of the barf pot in the kitchen. Then I came back and curled up next to him.

"Feel better?" I rubbed his back.

"Kind of . . . yeah, mostly. Just a little queasy." He stiffened. "Hey, you better get off. What if Mom—"

"She was meeting her friends for drinks after shopping. They're a bunch of alchies; she won't be home for hours." I smoothed his shirt, caressing him.

"We shouldn't take the chance."

My hands went lower, and under the shirt. I slid them around his stomach to the front.

"Sam, cut it out."

"Why? I want to make you feel better." To soothe him, even in some small way.

"You're turning into a sex addict. And we can't do anything until after eleven, Sam. You know that."

"Okay, okay." I moved to his back again. I wasn't a sex addict; it wasn't the sex I craved. It was the normalcy; when we were having sex, we were like everyone else. For just that little while, neither of us was dying.

"You've become so . . . aggressive," he said.

"You don't like that?" I lifted my hands.

"I do . . . I do."

I went back to massaging. What he saw as aggressive, I saw as making the best of each moment. But I didn't say it out loud; I didn't want to waste any time talking about it. So I just kept pressing into his back to make him feel better—and to touch him. Just to touch him, and not think, and be normal.

He said, "It's just—you're different."

"We weren't having sex before. Now we're *both* different." I kissed his head. "At least I got you to stop wearing that hat."

He turned around, groaning loudly. "I hope we did the right thing."

I stared into his eyes. *What does he mean? Does he regret sleeping with me? Am I not good enough? Does he wish he was with Cindy?* All these ugly questions swirled inside, but part of me knew enough to keep them bottled up. It knew not to give them a voice. Because what would happen if I did?

Jess took my hand, squeezed it.

He cares ... doesn't he? Not that I had any right to expect him to care. Sex was sex. I'd crawled into his bed, not vice versa. I'd done him a favor; but he owed me nothing in return. If I cared about him—God it hurt to even think this—if I cared about him more than I should, it was my own damn problem.

Maybe Jess didn't mean anything bad at all; maybe he was worried about me, like Maria.

Why does that thought bother me, too? All I wanted to do was quit thinking.

Jess was still holding my hand. It was so confusing—part of me wanted him to stop, and part of me wanted him to never let go. Like that was even possible.

I told him, "We did the only thing we could do."

"You ever think about your dad?" Jess asked me in the dark. It was midnight, but I wasn't sleeping; not even close.

"Of course," I said. "Every day." More than thinking of him, I'd see him. Hints of him, as brief as one inhaled breath. In the hallway, when the elevator doors opened, I'd catch a glimpse of his overcoat. Sunday mornings at the breakfast table, I'd see his hands holding the ends of *The New York Times* open wide. When I walked by Mom's room, I'd see his form under the covers on his side of the bed. Just for a moment, I'd see a piece of him; then he was gone.

"You don't talk about him." His voice was incredibly low.

"I guess I didn't think you wanted to hear it." Was it a ghost, or was it my mind? I had no way of knowing, and what did it matter anyway? Either way, I couldn't have him back.

"Hear what?"

"How much I miss him." I hated it. I hated seeing him for split seconds, then losing him again, over and over. *How can I tell Jess that?*

Jess sucked in air and let it out slowly. "There's where

you're wrong; not only do I *want* to know, but I *need* to know."

"Why?" What possible good would it do him to know how tortured I was? I did my best not to think about it myself—to shove my father's haunting of me into a hidden corner of my mind.

"'Cause what scares me the most about dying . . . more than being gone—" He took a breath. When he spoke again, his voice shook. "The worst thing is to be forgotten. Like I wasn't even here."

That snapped me out of my Hamlet-like thoughts; I sat up and turned on the light. "Jesse, I haven't forgotten my dad, and I'm not going to forget you."

"Maybe not in the beginning, but one day." He avoided my gaze, staring at the ceiling. "One day you'll have a family, and my pictures'll be packed up in a cardboard box in your attic, next to the Christmas decorations."

My eyes went to the snapshot on the bedside table: Jess and his friends at senior movie night. And me, too. Always with them—Samantha, the junior tagalong.

"That won't happen," I said, staring at the faces from the past. Innocent faces. Unaffected, unaware of what would come.

"You don't know—you can't promise that," he said.

Pete on one side of Jess, me on the other. No Miss Perfect Cindy Evans to annoy me, because she and Jess were in breakup mode. Our biggest problem was Pete and me getting on each other's nerves, each jealous of the other's closeness with Jess. So stupid and trivial, except who knew that at the time? Jagged cracks ran through our faces, mine and Pete's, like punishment; slaps for being so petty. Jess at the photo's center, his big smile unobliterated despite the crack running through it.

I looked over at Jess now. The broken Jess, fractured like the plastic frame. Stripped of his smile.

I answered him. "Yes, I can, and I do. You mean everything to me, Jess. Everything. No matter what, I'll always remember that."

He looked at me, a frightened little boy, vulnerable and alone. I blinked back the tears. I needed to be strong, for him. I kicked back my covers, got up, and climbed into his bed, reaching for him. He was shaking.

"I want to believe you," he said. "So much, I want to believe you."

I pressed into him with all my strength. "You can."

We lay like that for a while, not speaking. Then I told him about my dad. "It bothers me that I can never see his face," I said.

"How long has this been happening?"

"I don't know . . . not that long. A couple of months, I guess."

"Wow, I can't believe you never said anything before."

"I was afraid you'd think I was crazy." *Plus, there's the death thing I don't want to bring up.*

"I don't think you're crazy," Jess said, giving me a squeeze. "I think you're sad."

"Well, yeah." *What is there to be happy about?*

"What about you?" I asked him. "You think about your dad?"

"Dick?" Jess's voice turned angry. "Gee, what's there to think about a guy who likes to be called 'Dick'?"

"He's your father."

"Yeah, like Darth Vader is Luke Skywalker's: in sperm only." He gave a sharp laugh. "Hey, at least Darth was a good guy, once." He raised his eyebrows. "You think 'the dark side' made Dick like he is?"

"Oh, for God's sake, be serious." It was a hard subject for Jesse; that's why he made it a joke. "I still say you should call him."

"Yeah. That'd be a great conversation. 'Hey, Dad. Just wanted to let you know I'm dying, in case you care. Sorry I couldn't do it a little younger and save you some support checks.' Just terrific."

"Whatever."

Jesse took in a deep breath, then released it. I rose and fell with his chest. "Sam, he walked out on me and my mom. You don't get what that's like; you had a dad who loved you."

"You don't know that he doesn't love you."

"I don't want or need the kind of love that makes leaving and never looking back okay," he said. "He broke my mom's heart."

I hadn't thought of it like that; that must've sucked for Gwen. And even if she wasn't the greatest mom, at least she'd been there for Jess—as much as she was capable of.

"You're right," I told him. His father was a jerk, but what could be done about that? Nothing. Sometimes, the only answer was nothing. The hard thing was to find peace with that.

Only Jess could know if he'd done that, so I had to let it go.

Meanwhile, what I'd really wanted to bring up—what I couldn't bring myself to ask all night—was rising to the surface.

"Jess?"

"Yeah?"

"Maria told me Dr. Raab suggested some experimental treatments to you."

His body stiffened. "So?"

"She said you refused them."

"So?" He'd tightened up even more, so much so that I felt uncomfortable and even unwelcome lying on him.

I didn't move, though. Nor did I sway from the topic. "Why'd you do that?"

He didn't speak for a while.

I waited.

Finally he said, "I don't feel like being a guinea pig, some lab rat. I'm starting the radiation again—the return of lobster boy. That's enough."

It wasn't enough. "If the doctor thinks they're a good idea—"

He waved his free arm, all disgusted. "Ahhhggg . . . probably just more money for him. I'm sick of being a pin cushion for no reason." He gave me an angry peck and pulled away from me. "I'm tired. You'd better go back in your bed."

This is what sunk my heart, more than anything else. That he was just going to lie down and die.

Chapter 8

June already. Prom night for Midland Prep at Tavern on the Green—for everyone except Jesse.

He could have gone. Everyone in school missed him. His friends called, especially Pete, but he still wouldn't talk to them. He always said no to visits. It might have been embarrassment, partly. I'm sure he didn't want his pals to see him bald and unable to walk much. But it was more the other thing: he didn't want to be reminded of what he'd lost.

I couldn't let the night just go by. So two days before the prom, after school, I went shopping. Friday afternoon I made some preparations. And then I showed him my surprise.

"What's this?" he asked, his voice stone cold.

"What does it look like? It's a tux."

He slammed his hands on the bar, gripping hard. "You know I'm not going to the prom!"

"No, I know. I'm taking you out—just us."

"I don't want to go anywhere, Sam."

I'd expected some resistance. "Hey, I worked hard on this."

"I don't want to sit in some restaurant—"

"No restaurant."

"Or club—"

"No club."

"Or any place packed with people—"

"No people."

His eyebrows raised. "No people?"

I came over and rested my hand over his tight, white knuckles. "Just us."

His grip relaxed. "Where can we go in New York City where it'll be just us?"

I gave his hand a final squeeze and headed for the door. "Put your tux on. I'm going home to get ready."

"Sam—"

"Trust me, okay? I'm going to show you a good time."

He looked doubtful. "I guess you can try."

"Oh, Samantha!" Mom put her hand to her mouth. "You look beautiful."

I felt ridiculous. I never even put on lipstick, and here I was in pink satin and taffeta, rhinestone belt and earrings, and pearl necklace. Full prom throttle. "Can you help me do my hair?"

"You know how long I've waited for you to ask?"

"Sam!" Teddy yanked on my hemline. "Sam!" He pointed to my pink pumps. "Can I borrow those shoes sometime?"

"Sure, Teddy."

Mom and I went into her room, and I sat in front of the mirror. She brushed my hair out. "Baby?"

"Yeah?" I was fascinated by my made-up face—the reflection of a stranger.

"I thought Jesse didn't want to go to his prom."

"We're not going to the prom."

"Then where are you going?"

"I'm taking him somewhere else."

"Where?"

"Don't worry about it."

"Don't worry about it?" Her voice had a sudden sharp edge. She swiveled my chair around. "You're my seventeen-year-old daughter. You sleep in a boy's room every night. And I'm not supposed to ask any questions?"

"It's not just any boy. It's Jesse." God, that wall was back.

"You're sleeping with him."

"Mom!" I couldn't take the stare.

"Sammy, can I borrow your shoes now?" Teddy bounced into the room, dancing around.

"Teddy, go play in your room," Mom said. "Samantha and I are talking."

"But, but—"

"*Go!*"

Teddy ran from the room; Mom probably had never raised her voice to him before. She leaned into my face. "You and Jesse are having sex, aren't you?"

"No."

"Don't lie to me, Sam. We've always told each other the truth—always."

I stared at carpet fibers.

"I write about sex for a living, honey. I know all the signs."

The fibers were really fluffy.

"Samantha!"

"Okay, okay! Yes! Is that what you want to hear?"

"Oh, God." She sank on to her bed and covered her eyes.

"I'm not going to stop. I don't care what you say."

Mom's hands dropped from her face. She stared at me with eyes suddenly cold. "Convenient, isn't it? For Jesse, to have his best friend to *comfort* him."

I sucked in air, unable to speak. *How can she say that? How can she think that Jess would use me?* But then, it wasn't like Jess had ever thought of dating me before, either.

The room spun around me, filled with the awful thoughts my mother had conjured. If I hadn't been sitting already, I'd probably have fallen. I sat frozen, paralyzed by implication and fear, until I felt warm pressure on my shoulders. Mom was there, in front of me, holding me.

"I'm sorry, Sam. I didn't mean to upset you." I felt her take a deep breath and let it out. Time seemed timeless as her heart pounded against me, through my pink silk. "I understand," she said finally. Her voice was warm now, like her touch. She pulled back a little, looked into my eyes softly. She was Mom again. My terrors retreated back into the shadows.

"You do?"

She nodded. "But I'm worried about what's going to happen to you."

I paused for a moment before answering, trying to make sure all the bad feelings were gone. "I'll be all right."

"You think you know the answers, but—"

"I don't know the answers." God, that was the truth. "I just know that me and Jess, we need to be together—as long as we can be."

She looked like she wanted to say something but couldn't piece it together. Finally, she laughed. "I'm sending my teenage daughter off to have sex. It's official: I'm nuts."

I was still feeling shook up, but I forced out a smile. "You're sending your daughter off to be with her best friend. *Period*."

She clutched my hands for a bit. Then, letting go, she said, "C'mon, let's finish that hair."

Chapter 9

"Going somewhere with my son?"

Jesus, it was round two, and Gwen gave me the big stare-down. She'd intercepted me on the way to Jesse's room.

I tried looking around her. "Yeah."

"I've never seen you so . . . feminine before."

I shrugged.

"Are you two dating now?"

"We're just going out on prom night, Ma." Jesse came up behind her. "We're playing dress-up; it's a game."

"Jesse! You look wonderful!" She stared at him, and so did I. He looked smokin' in his black tux with purple bow tie. And no hat.

Thank God he was running interference for me. He pecked Gwen on the cheek. "See ya, Mom." He brushed past her and gave me a push, nudging me out before Gwen thought of something else obnoxious to say.

"Hey, hot stuff," he said in the elevator, leaning against the back handrail. "Lookin' good!" He hit the Stop button and grabbed me, kissing me hard and deep, even as I supported his weight. Then he started the elevator moving again.

"You've sure changed your mood."

"How can I be grumpy in a tux?" He held on to me with one hand, and with the other he gave me a squeeze on the tush. "And with you looking like that?"

Ding! We hit ground.

Outside, I took him by the arm and led him across the street. "Where we going?" he asked.

"I told you, it's a surprise."

"Don't we need a cab?"

"No." I opened my little satin purse and pulled out a black scarf—the only thing in there besides a condom.

"What are you doin' with that?"

"Blindfolding you."

"Kinky." He bent to let me tie it around his eyes. "I wouldn't trust anyone else to lead me off like this, Sam."

I took his hand and led him slowly into the park.

"Whatcha doin'?" Jesse asked. I'd left him standing, still blindfolded, while I set up everything. I'd hidden it all behind the bushes earlier in the day.

"Ready?" I pulled off the scarf. We were standing in the spot where we used to picnic—Mom and us, or Maria and us. A patch of grass surrounded by shrubs and three tall, leafy trees.

It was where we used to play tag, and hide-and-seek, and other kid games. It was where Jesse tackled me, making me taste dirt through my laughter. It was where we made up stories about what we were going to do when we grew up; it was where we learned to dream.

"Omigod," he said, staring at the white lights strung all through the bushes. "How'd you light them?"

"Portable generator. Let's hope our building doesn't have a blackout, because I borrowed it from Manny." It paid to be nice to the maintenance guy.

He looked at the checkered blanket with place settings for two. In the center was a roasted chicken, grilled vegetables, sparkling cider, and apple pie—Jesse loved apple pie. "This is as gourmet as I get," I said.

"It's perfect."

He seemed so happy, but then, in a fraction of a second, his spark extinguished. "Sam, why'd you bring me here?"

The thought had been building for months, that if I could just get Jesse back into the park—if I could just get Jesse to allow the park back in—then maybe I could get him to hope . . . to fight.

"I'm sorry," I said softly. It suddenly hit me that I was wrong to push him, to force him to go where he didn't want to be. It was his life, after all. "I wanted you to remember the good times we had here."

He didn't say anything, just shuffled his shiny black shoes in the grass. Then he looked all around again, staring at the twinkly lights that made me feel like I was on heaven's threshold. His smile came back.

He kissed me, ran his fingers down the side of my neck. "Thanks."

We sat on the blanket and ate. It was a beautiful, clear night. The kind where you couldn't imagine anything being wrong in the world.

"Oh, I almost forgot," I said, swooshing taffeta as I got up.

I hit Play on the iPod, and Abba sang to us: "Does your mother know that you're out?"

He hoisted himself up. "Care to dance?" he asked, putting his arms around me. I nestled into his chest, tucking my head under his chin and holding him tight. It felt so good, his body pitched against me. I could stay there always. I listened to his heart beat: *Thump. Thump. Thump.*

Abba was warning me to take it easy. Easy to say, wasn't it. But taking it easy didn't seem within my capacity these days. Tears welled in my eyes; I sniffled.

He looked at me. "What's wrong?"

"I feel so bad," I said, tears rubbing into his white shirt. Guilt prickled through my body, goading my tears. *How can I be so happy when Jess shouldn't be here at all?* "You belong somewhere else," I told him.

"No I don't."

"You do." He would have been king of the prom—I was sure. "If you could take any girl to the prom tonight, who would it be? Cindy Evans, I bet." That was an almost sure thing. Other girls who'd been hot for Jess paraded through my mind. "Or Elyse Carmichael. Or Jamie Sut-houser. Or Valerie Daniels . . ."

I had no right, but I felt jealous just then; jealous of the girl who would've been in Jesse's arms if he hadn't gotten sick. I couldn't be sure who it would've been, but it would-n't have been me. I could picture them in silhouette, danc-ing under a dazzling rainbow of swirling spotlights while the band played Dido. I could see him pulling her closer, closer. I could see their mouths touching. . . .

Jess pressed his finger on my cheek and stared into me, yanking me from my solitary spot by the punch bowl at Tavern on the Green.

God. Those eyes.

Those eyes—they looked right inside.

"I'd take the girl next door." Jess's voice was hushed, sincere. He inhaled air in deep bursts, like he was making up for the breath he took from me.

The sky seemed magnified through all my tears. The stars flickered wildly, like the lights on Broadway. *Please*, I begged them silently, squeezing my eyes shut. *Please don't take Jesse away.*

His lips dug into mine, wet and desperate.

Chapter 10

We made love right there, on the checkered blanket. Just shoved the glasses and plates aside and did it in the cool air while Abba sang on.

"So how do you feel?" I asked afterward. We were spread out on the blanket, staring at the stars. My head lay against Jesse's chest and I fiddled with his bow tie.

"Not to be crude, but I just got laid. I feel great."

"Oh, stop. I meant, how do you feel being here?"

"Hmmm . . ." He traced his finger across my pearls. "I guess I'm relieved. I was so full of anger and self-pity. It was like I centered it all in this park; I had to shut myself off, shut myself out, to get away from the hurt."

"And now?"

His hand was under the necklace, tickling. "And now . . . I feel light. Like everything's been lifted."

I rolled over to face him. "You have room for something else now?"

"What?"

"Hope."

He looked back up at the sky. "Why would I want to hope? Just to inject myself with a fresh dose of pain?"

"You can fight it, Jesse." The tears started coming again. "Please."

"Sam, no one with a dual translocation survives."

"There's a chance—"

"It's easier to accept it."

"When did you get to be such a wimp?"

"Hey, you try it." His voice was sharp. "Being on top of the world, then getting flicked off the globe without warning. Squashed like a bug by the hand of God."

"You think God did this to you?"

He clutched a fistful of blanket. "Who the fuck knows. Doesn't matter; it's done, I'm dying. Deal with it."

"I thought you let go of your anger."

He looked at me with lost eyes and burst into tears. I grabbed his lapel and clung to him like he was hanging from a cliff.

"Jesse, say what's inside."

He slobbered on my neck, heaving sobs, sounding almost inhuman.

"Say it, Jesse." I knew—I knew there was a fighter in there somewhere.

"Leave me alone! Just let me be," he shrieked. My arms were roped around his waist under his jacket and tight against his back. He tried to pull free but I held on. He pounded his fist into my arm; my flesh and muscle lit with cramping agony, but I still wouldn't let go.

"No more pain; I can't take any more pain," he wailed.

We were covered in each other's tears. Mascara ran

into my eyes, burning and blurring everything black. Jess shook like he was just yanked from a hole in the middle of a frozen lake.

"Jesse, Jesse . . . " I choked on his name.

Then he let out a high-pitched wail: "Oh, God!" He clawed into my back. "Oh, God, I don't want to die!"

"Oh my God, Sam. I hit you. I'm a fucking animal." It was the first thing he'd said in about an hour. He'd spent the minutes crying into the poufy satin shoulder of my dress, stopping briefly, then crying some more.

"It doesn't matter, Jess."

"Yes it does matter. I'm a goddamn batterer." He examined the black and blue mark on my arm.

"I provoked you." He touched the bruise and I winced. He looked horrified.

"That's just what a battered woman would say. I'm a fucking wife beater!"

"I'm not your wife."

"Thank God! I'd probably beat the crap out of you."

"Stop it, Jesse. I pushed you and you snapped. You'd never hurt me otherwise. I know that."

"How do you know? It always starts with one good sock, then the scumbag's full of remorse—until the next time."

"You're not a scumbag. You're just an emotional wreck."

"You going to tell your mom?"

"No!"

"See! You're covering up, just like a battered woman already. Shit."

"You need to chill out, dude." I held my palm up. "Don't make me slap you."

He stared at my hand. "Jeez, maybe you're a beater, too."

"Maybe."

That made us both laugh. He lay back on the blanket and I followed, completely wiped.

He kissed me. "Thanks, Sam."

"For what? For giving you the most fucked-up, miserable prom night ever?"

"You know for what." He kissed me more deeply. "For playing therapist."

"Was I any good at it?"

"I'll lie on your couch anytime." He sucked on my neck, giving me goose bumps. Then a thought hit—the doubt. But it was too late to do anything but lay guilt on me. Had I helped Jess, or just brought more heartache to the surface? What did I know? Half the time I felt like I was ready for the psych ward myself.

"I'll do the experimental treatment." Jess's voice tickled inside my ear, almost unbearably. "For you, Sam—I'd do anything for you."

For me? What about for him? Didn't he even remotely believe the treatment would work? But I couldn't ask him then; it was enough for one night. And did it matter why he was doing it anyway? The important thing was, he was doing it. *Right?*

I almost said something more, but before I could string the words together he spoke.

"Back to the party." Jess hauled himself up and turned on the iPod player again. Then he reached for me and helped me up. "C'mon, let's dance."

Abba serenaded us as we swayed under the stars. You had to get in a good mood when "Dancing Queen" came on—the slide of the piano keys was an instant spirit lifter.

Leaning on me, Jess nibbled on my earlobe, then breathed the heated words inside my ear: "I love you."

Chapter 11

A few days later I came home from school to find Jess using his laptop—something I hadn't seen in a long time.

"What up," I said casually, not wanting to make a big deal that he was doing something other than vegetating.

"Dr. Raab told me there's some sites for young adults with cancer," Jess said. "He thought I could find some people to chat with . . . you know, with the same stuff going on."

"Cool," I said. "Great idea. So, you find anyone?"

"I found a bunch of anyones," he said with a laugh. "I'm just reading through the threads right now. I'm not quite ready to take the plunge into posting."

"You do that, and I'll get some homework done," I said, relieved that he was occupied with something for once. It was hard studying when I felt like I needed to keep his spirits up all the time. I felt bad enough leaving him alone all day. But I did have a chemistry final in two days; cracking that book might be a smart idea. I unzipped my backpack and hauled the hefty thing out.

"Yeah, about studying," Jess said.

I looked up from the book. "What about it?"

"You should go to summer school," he said.

"No way."

"You're messing up your life, Sam."

I slammed the book shut and shoved it, a little too hard, sending it over the edge of the bed. "Okay, when did my mom come talk to you?"

"Today, while you were at school." He propped up his head with his arm and leaned sideways at me. "She's right, you know."

"Yeah?"

"Yeah." He crossed his ankles. "It's not good for you to spend so much time in this room."

"Then let's go out more."

"I mean, you need to be around other people."

I waved the ridiculous suggestion away without comment.

"Sam, what's going to happen to you—really?"

My heart raced at the words. *No more questions. Please, no more questions.*

I didn't answer.

He said, "I care about you too much not to talk about this."

I still didn't answer.

"Don't look at me like that, Sam. I agreed to try and fight. I'm starting the stem cell clinical trial Dr. Raab kept yapping about, aren't I? But we have to be realistic."

Why?

"Your mom's afraid you're going to stick a knife in

77

your stomach and throw yourself over my dead body like in some twisted version of *Romeo and Juliet*."

I didn't say anything; the thought had crossed my mind.

"Well?"

I turned away from him, fixing my eyes once again on that picture on the bedside table—the snapshot of lost smiles and lost people. Why hadn't I appreciated the simple life we had, a friendship some people never found? *Why had I wanted more?* God, it was almost like I'd willed his illness, so I could have him to myself.

"Sam, I'm waiting for you to tell me you're not going to stick a knife in your stomach and throw yourself over my dead body like in some twisted version of *Romeo and Juliet*."

Silence.

"Hello!"

Finally I turned to him. "We're not even boyfriend and girlfriend."

"We're not?"

My eyebrows narrowed together. "Why? You think we are?"

"I don't know, Miss Sex Kitten. I could've sworn it was you in this bed with me."

"That's just sex."

"Oh, excuse me." He was red now, like his temperature was rising. "And it meant nothing to you when I told you I loved you in the park?"

I stared at him. "I thought you meant it like—like al-

ways. I mean, we've—we've always loved . . . each other."
I was tripping over the words.

"I didn't know I needed to formally ask you out," he
snapped. "I thought it was obvious I meant the *other* kind
of love."

"I—I—I—" I was real smooth.

"I kind of got the feeling you were falling in love with
me, too. But I guess I was wrong."

"Yeah, you were wrong," I said, shoving myself off the
bed. "Because I was in love with you long before we ever
had sex." I couldn't look at him. I just headed for the door.
"Years," I added, gripping the handle. I closed the door behind me and leaned against it, wiping tears from my eyes.
I'd never admitted that before, even to myself.

God, love is draining.

So now I had what I'd never dared think of. Why did I
feel so damn heartbroken?

I ran out of Jesse's apartment, through the Emerald
City. There's no place like home. . . . I didn't have my key,
and I leaned on the bell, letting it ring and ring as my tears
rained onto our welcome mat.

Mom swung the door open. "Baby, what's wrong?"

I fell into her arms, sobbing. "Is it Jesse?" she asked,
hugging me tightly.

I couldn't give a clear answer. The words came out gar-
bled.

"Sam? Is Jesse okay?"

I nodded yes, pressing into her shoulder. I felt her cheek against the top of my hair.

"Did you have a fight?"

I nodded yes again; I coughed, choking on tears.

"Come lie down. Your brother's sleeping over at his friend Ben's apartment, thank goodness. I think he's seen enough, don't you?"

She led me down the hall and into my room. My bed creaked as I climbed onto it, and again when Mom lay next to me. "Do you want to tell me about it?"

"He said—he said—" I blubbered out tears and the words were bogged in saliva. "He said he loves me."

"And?"

"That's it. He's in love with me." I grabbed a patchwork pillow and clutched it against me, tracing the stitching with my hands.

"And this upsets you?"

A sob burst from my throat. "Yeah. I don't know why, but it's like . . ." My voice quavered. "It's like the saddest thing ever."

"I don't understand, baby." She stroked my hair.

"I—I don't either. It's just that I loved him for *sooo* long. . . ." I stopped to take a deep breath. "And now, when he's so sick, *now* he loves me back?"

"Maybe he loved you all along, too. Maybe he just didn't know it." She kissed my forehead. "You guys are so young."

"But I knew."

"When it comes to love, sweetheart, guys are generally years behind girls."

"S—S—Sam . . ." Jesse's faint voice startled us. He was leaning in the door frame, clutching it for support and gasping for breath.

Mom and I rushed over and got him. We each took an arm and guided him to the bed. It creaked again as we helped him lie on the quilt. He was wheezing like an asthmatic, and his heart was doing laps.

"Jesse, should we call 911?" Mom asked.

He just kept gasping and coughing.

God, what have I done to him?

"Jesse," Mom repeated. She grabbed his face and held it. "Look at me. Should I call an ambulance?"

He shook his head no. "Maria—," he managed before another coughing fit.

"You need Maria?" she asked.

He nodded. "Oxy—"

"He wants his oxygen mask," I said. I started to go get it, but his hand shot up and grabbed my wrist.

"St—stay," he said.

"I'll go," Mom said. There were tears in her eyes now as she sprinted out.

Jesse pulled at my wrist. He wanted me to sit next to him. My butt caused more creaking. "S—sorry," he panted. "S—stupid me . . ." His chest heaved up and down, up and down, up and down.

I started to cry again. I knew I should have controlled myself, I knew I should have been helping him, but it was all too much.

"I—" He pushed out the word slowly, like a dying old man. "I—I—" He choked hard, and I pulled him up, afraid he couldn't breathe lying down. Then he fell against me, still making horrible sounds.

"Jesus Chris'! Whatsamatta?" Maria bellowed as she burst in, carrying the portable oxygen tank and mask. Mom was right behind her, completely pale.

I tried to get up and out of the way, but Jess clung to me like a life raft in the sea.

Maria slipped the mask over his nose and mouth, pulling the elastic behind his ears. She gave him a gentle push. "Lie back, Jesse. Lie back an' breathe slow, okay?"

He held on to me and I sank onto the bed with him. He was still making choking noises. "Clos' you eyes and relax, Jesse. Breathe deep. Be calm," Maria said. His chest was still heaving and he squeezed into my arms, trembling.

"Jess, please. Please listen to Maria," I begged.

His fingers dug into my flesh. He tried to speak and couldn't with the mask on. But his eyes were pleading.

"I'm not going to leave, Jess. I'll stay here all night with you. Just please, calm down."

"Jesse," Maria said again, "jus' relax and breathe. Put everythin' outta your head, unless you wanna go ta da hospital. I'm gonna call 911 in a minute if you no betta."

His eyes closed, his breathing slowed; he was coughing and wheezing less and less. Finally, thank God, he was just breathing. He turned a little and opened his eyes, looking at me with this incredible love. A serenity flowed through me, and I felt completely calm.

Maybe I'd read one too many of Mom's novels.

Jesse's eyes flickered, then shut. "Good, he's restin' now," Maria said to my mom.

They were beside us, watching, both with deep worry on their faces. Then they got blurry; I shifted, burrowing myself comfortably against Jesse, and my eyelids dropped shut.

I felt my mom kiss my cheek somewhere in the distance as I fell asleep. "Love you, baby."

I wanted to tell her I loved her, too; but I was already miles away.

With Jesse.

Chapter 12

I woke up in the dark, my mouth tasting like sandpaper. My head lay against Jesse's chest and his heart thumped, loud—in normal time, thank God. I felt his face: the mask was off. Maria must have taken it away after I fell asleep. He was in a deep sleep now. I smoothed my hand over his T-shirt, down his stomach.

God, I loved him. I pecked his forehead and got out of bed.

I'd fallen asleep in my sneakers. I kicked them off, felt the plush area rug under my feet. Opening my door slowly, I slipped out sideways, trying not to let too much light into the room, and blinked, adjusting my eyes.

Voices were coming from my living room. I went into the bathroom and drank a glass of water. Then I crept down the bare-wood hallway and pressed myself against the wall between the doorway and the gold-framed painting of tulips.

Gwen was hammering my mom. "You didn't even *call* me. And Maria didn't contact me until an *hour* after it happened!"

"Sorry. We were more concerned about Jesse's welfare than with prying your lips from your martini glass."

"How dare you! My son had some sort of panic attack and you didn't think it important enough . . . ?"

"Listen, Gwen. Maria and I stood watch by Jesse for an hour after he fell asleep to make sure he was okay. *That's* why it took so long for her to call you. And I'll tell you something else: if *my* child had terminal cancer, I wouldn't need to be called if there was an emergency. I'd already *be* there."

"So you think you know what it's like . . . ?"

"No, I don't know what it's like, Gwen. But do *you* know that Sam cuts school to go with Jesse to his treatments?"

"I'm not surprised. She's become more and more uncontrollable."

"She doesn't want him to go through it by himself. Tell me, why is it that his own *mother* sends him off with a car service, instead of going with him?"

"Don't you judge me!"

Mom's voice toned down a smidge, but it was still firm. "I don't judge people. But you asked why I didn't call you. You leave your dying son alone, to face his demons daily, so you can soak your liver in alcohol. Who'd expect you'd ever come running?"

There was a long silence. Then Gwen spoke. "He doesn't want me there."

"Excuse me?"

"He doesn't want me with him at the treatments. That's why I don't go."

"He's told you this?"

"No, no. It's just . . . he's so sarcastic when he speaks to me. He's got this coldness in his voice." Gwen's voice was so low, it was barely audible. "He hates me."

"He doesn't hate you, Gwen. He's afraid, that's all. Terror makes people behave badly. He hates what's happening to him, not you. When your husband walked out, you were scared, weren't you? Jesse felt like you didn't care about him because of your behavior, but you did care, didn't you?"

"I loved—I love him so much." I remembered that day, when Gwen said she cared about Jess as she was headed for the door, and how he hadn't heard her. Why hadn't I told him? God, I'd been so wrapped up in my own drama, I'd forgotten to tell him. *So selfish, so self-absorbed.*

"You can still tell him, Gwen," Mom said. "It's not too late. I don't think it's ever too late. I tell my husband I love him all the time."

Huh. Suddenly I wondered if I was the only one having visions of my dad. But I didn't get a chance to think much about that because Gwen asked the questions I'd been dreading: "What was he doing here anyway? What brought this all on?"

Don't tell her, don't tell her, I begged silently.

"The kids had a fight; Sam ran out and he came after her. He probably tried to move too fast—and he was upset." My mother cannot tell a lie.

Gwen sighed. "All right; I've had enough. I'm sending your daughter packing."

No!

"No, Gwen, you're not." Mom's voice wasn't nasty, but it was firm. It left no room for argument.

Mom went on, "You should thank God Jesse has Sam, and that he's had her all these years. I know you've had your issues, and I know you love him. But the sad thing is, I doubt he knows it. Don't you think he deserves to have someone with him he's *sure* cares?"

Gwen made a choking sound; I couldn't make out what it meant, if she was trying to say something, or what.

"Are you all right?" Mom asked her. "You're very flushed."

"I'm fine—I just feel a little dizzy."

"Do you want some water?"

Uh-oh. I got ready to run.

"No. I—" She let out a long sigh. "I just don't know how everything went so wrong."

Mom didn't say anything. There was nothing to say, really. People usually know exactly where things went wrong. It's just easier to pretend that they don't.

"May I see Jesse, please?" Gwen's voice was quiet again, and really sad.

"Of course."

I rushed back to my room and climbed in next to Jesse, shutting my eyes.

I heard Mom and Gwen walk in. "May I sit by him?"

"Sure. I'll get the chair for you."

Gwen's body moved in next to Jesse. Her breath sounded heavy.

"I'll leave you alone," Mom said.

This was creepy, in the dark with Gwen, and Jesse asleep.

She made a strange noise, a sucking-in kind of sound. Then sharp, staggered gulps. *Is Gwen crying?*

I had to peek.

The door was cracked open, allowing a beam of light in. It was enough to see the tears—and something else: Gwen was holding Jesse's hand.

I woke to lips pressing all over my face. "Forgive me, Sam," Jess said, between kisses.

Forgive him? I nearly killed him yesterday.

"It was my fault. I sent you into convulsions."

He stroked my hair. "Are we okay now?"

I nodded. "Are *you* okay?"

"I feel tired, that's all. And I had this crazy dream that my mom was holding my hand. Talk about a long shot."

"That wasn't a dream."

"What?"

"It wasn't a dream. Gwen was holding your hand. She was crying, too."

"What?" he asked again.

"Shocking, I know. And there's more." I told him what I'd heard last night, and what I'd heard Gwen say months ago when she was leaving his room.

"Wow," he said. He tilted away from me and sniffed. I

turned his head back toward me and faced the tears. We'd never really talked about his mom's behavior, in all this time.

"It wasn't you, Jess. It was her. She sees it, now—that she was wrong." He tried to look past me, toward my desk, but I grabbed his face again; I was going to be there for him whether he liked it or not.

And he didn't like it. "Sam, just leave me alone for a while, okay?"

"You mean that?"

He hesitated. "It isn't right, you picking up my pieces all the time. It's supposed to be the other way around."

"Macho idiot," I said. I leaned against him. "You glued me back together two and a half years ago, remember? So let me have my turn."

"Fine," he croaked as his tears erupted, saturating my shirt. "If you insist."

There was a rap at my bedroom door. "Come in," I called. Jess was lying against me, red-eyed, sniffling a little.

The door opened and Mom stuck her face in. "How are you guys doing?"

"We're okay," I said.

She stepped in all the way and looked at Jess. "Are you feeling all right?"

"Yeah," he said with a stuffy voice. "Mrs. Everfield,

I'm really sorry about the trouble I caused you last night."
He looked away.

Mom came closer. "Number one, Jesse: how many
years do I have to tell you to call me Ellen? Number two,
there's no reason to apologize. Nothing you can ever do
will cause me trouble. I'm just glad you're feeling better."
She smiled. "I made breakfast. Do you want it in the dining
room, or in here?"

"I'll get up," Jesse said. "Got to do it sometime, right?"
He looked around the room, and then settled his eyes on
Mom. "Although I wouldn't mind sticking around here for
a while."

"You can always use this as your oasis, Jesse." She
gave him a kiss, and then me. "You too, Sam."

Ha ha, Mom.

"Just a warning, though. Teddy's home, and he's in a
real bouncy mood."

"That's cool. Maybe he can pass some bounce my
way," Jesse said.

"Well, breakfast—and Teddy—are ready whenever
you are." Mom smiled again and left.

"Jess, you go ahead. I want to get changed."

Jesse laughed. "You kidding me? We sleep together.
You can't get dressed in front of me?"

"My mom's outside. I don't feel right changing with
you in here."

"Yeah, okay. I didn't think about that." He lurched out
of my bed with a groan. "I'll see you in a few."

I pawed through my drawers, looking for God knows
what, because my spring wardrobe was simple—jeans,

90

sweats, and T-shirts, pretty interchangeable. But my mind wasn't focusing on the clothes. It was more like I was digging through my life, trying to find something to salvage, something to hold on to. I couldn't lose the feeling that I was a paper doll, just like Mom and me used to make, and someone was ripping, shredding me into pieces.

Without taking anything out, I shoved the drawer shut so hard that the stupid knickknacks cluttering the top of the dresser shook. These were what I was left with, useless tokens: the purple ceramic kitten, the porcelain eggs, the shell collection. The angel figurines with their mocking faces. I'd thought they were so important when I'd put them all there. Now I hated them all.

I swept them all to the floor. Since my area rug didn't reach to the dresser, everything fell onto hard wood. It felt damn good hearing all that crashing. Then I fell onto my knees, right on top of the rubble. On top of the broken ceramic kitty and the pulverized porcelain eggs, and the fractured shells and everything else. The pieces ground into my sweats, stabbing into my knees. And it felt good. It felt good to have destroyed those ridiculous trinkets.

"Sam, Sam." Jesse's arms were around me from behind, and I didn't even know how they got there. His head brushed the side of my hair. "Sweetheart, get up."

But I couldn't. I was too busy sifting my fingers through the grainy, glorious ruins.

"Baby?" Mom called from the doorway. I didn't answer. "Jesse, what's wrong with her?"

"Mommy, Mommy, let me through. I want to see what made all that noise," Teddy whined.

I wouldn't look away from my thrilling, gritty mess.

"Just keep Teddy out of here," Jesse said. "I'll take care of her."

"Jesse—" Mom's voice shook. Why couldn't I care? All that mattered was examining the shards, making sure every single thing had been smashed.

"I've got her, Ellen," he said softly; he had such a sweet voice. But I couldn't think about anything except my work. Had to make sure I got everything. . . .

"Lemme see! Lemme see!" my brother said, right before the door closed.

"Sam, we have to get up now," Jesse said into my ear.

I didn't say anything; I just kept shifting broken shards through my fingers and pressing my knees into the debris, mashing it more.

Jesse picked up a purple ear. "Why'd you do this? I gave you this kitten on your tenth birthday. Remember? And the glass tulip . . ." He pinched a red shimmering sliver between his fingers. "Your dad brought this back from Holland that time."

It was true. Everything on that dresser came from my dad or Jesse. It was like I'd created a shrine to them or something. I didn't remember separating out their gifts and souvenirs, but I had. Even the shells. I'd found them with my dad along the beach on Long Island. The harvest of years of summer collecting. . . .

"I don't understand," Jesse said, leaning his chin on my head. He pulled me tight against him, trying to make me feel better. But the satisfaction was in the rubble I crunched through, still.

"What good are objects?" I spat the words out through my dry mouth, leaning forward and swiping my hand into the fragments. "What good are keepsakes when you can't keep the people?"

Jesse pulled me away from the wreckage and inched me backward across the carpet a few feet. I didn't fight him; I didn't have the strength. But I didn't help him, either.

He huffed, slowly dragging both our bodies, one arm around me and his other on the floor. He stopped at the beanbag chair.

"Sam, what is it?" he asked, squeezing my bloody hand. "What's going on?"

I giggled.

"What's so funny?"

I stared at the devastation I'd spawned, laughter bubbling from me.

"Jesus Christ, I've driven you insane," Jesse said.

I uncurled my hand and traced the powder mixed with blood in my palm and just kept laughing. . . .

Chapter 13

My chest ached when I finally snapped out of my trance, still propped in Jesse's arms. He had his legs wrapped over mine, pressed hard on my knees, and he held my palms against his thighs. I guessed he was stopping the bleeding.

"Jess?"

"Yeah?"

"What are you doin'?"

"Just waiting. Waiting for you to come back. I didn't know what else to do."

I turned around. There was so much I wanted to say. And yet there was nothing to say.

He checked one of my hands, touched the bloodied scratches on my palm, and kissed it. "Sam. I—I—" He paused, gulped. "I'm killing you, too. Aren't I? I'm taking you down with me."

"No, yes—I don't know," I said. "It's just—seeing you like that last night. It made everything even clearer. There's nothing I can do to stop what's happening to you. But why? Why can't I help you? Save you?"

"You help me more than anyone else," he said quietly.

"But it's not enough," I snapped.

The door opened and Mom came in. "Sam, what happened?" Her voice had a panicked edge.

"I . . . went nuts, kind of, I guess," I said.

"Let me look at you. Are you bleeding?"

Jess released my legs. There were dark sticky patches over both knees; I pulled up the sweat legs gingerly and we checked my knees. They looked pretty gruesome, but the bleeding had stopped from Jesse's pressure. Mom looked at the cuts on my palms, too.

"All right, we'll get you cleaned and bandaged, and that should be good enough. I don't think you need any stitches."

"Is Ted okay?" I asked.

"I have no idea. I guess we'll find out in a few years."

I looked at my feet. "Sorry, Mom."

"Aw, baby, I didn't mean that." She sat next to us and gave me a hug. "Everything's getting to me, too."

"Where is he?" I asked.

"Believe it or not, he's in the other room—with Gwen."

"Jeez, we'd better get him out of there before he really needs therapy," Jess said.

"What's she doing here?" I asked.

"She wants to talk to Jesse." Mom turned to him and said, "Your mother was here last night. She was very worried about you. I thought you'd like to know that."

Jesse didn't say anything.

"Jesse, she seems different, somehow." Mom frowned,

like she was thinking of the right way to put it, but couldn't. "I don't know. You can see for yourself."

He shifted a little, shuffled his feet back and forth. He had an edgy look.

"One more thing," Mom said, eyeing me. "Sam, I made an appointment for you to see a psychologist—this afternoon at four."

"Mom!"

"Don't you 'mom' me. You're lucky I don't have you under observation at Bellevue after what you just did. You're going! It's not up for debate."

"I want Jesse to come with me."

"He can go with you to the appointment, but he has to wait outside."

"No. I want him inside with me."

"I think he's been inside you enough. Dear God, I can't believe I just said that." Mom turned pink, I felt red, and Jesse looked kind of purple. "Okay, you know what I mean. You're having your session alone."

She looked at Jesse, who was trying to avoid looking back at her. "Jesse . . . oh, don't look so embarrassed. I made a Freudian slip, that's all. Anyway, you can understand it, can't you? Therapy is something that needs to be done solo."

He nodded.

"Thank you. You can sit with her for a few minutes when she first goes in, but then I want you to leave the room, even if she asks you to stay. Will you do that for me?"

He nodded.

"Okay! Sam, clean yourself up, and come have breakfast. We'll bandage you afterward. Jesse, go speak with your mother in the living room so we don't have to explain this latest fiasco, and then you can join us."

Something strange had happened to Mom's voice. Her pitch had risen, and her words sped up; she sounded like a frantic mouse. "Does that sound like a plan?" She was trying so hard to hold it together. And to her, that meant everyone getting a good meal.

"Yeah, Mom," I said softly. "That's a great plan. I'll be there in a minute, okay?"

"Yup!" The word popped out and Mom left almost as quickly. I hoped she'd chill out on her own; I didn't want to bring her to the therapist, too.

"Mom's buggin'," I said when she left.

"You *told* her we were having sex?" Jess was buggin', too. "Is that a lesser offense than dressing in front of me?"

"I wouldn't have sex with you *here*." It was all about respect. "She figured it out and asked me. I don't lie to my mom."

"Terrific."

"It's okay. She didn't yell at you or anything, did she? She's cool with it."

"I doubt that," he grumbled. "I feel funny as hell now. I don't know how I can face her again."

"Jess." I rubbed my hand on his leg. "She understands. She's on our side."

Jesse took a deep breath in and let it out; he grabbed a pillow and squeezed it. "Well, she's your mom. I guess if you want to talk to her about stuff, I can't blame you."

"It's not like I asked her how to have sex, for God's sake." Although I *had* used her books for guidelines.

"I know, I'm not mad. It's just a shock, that's all. And I'm always amazed—"

"By what?"

"By how nice your mom is. You're so lucky." He stared at my rubble.

"Maybe your mom'll be different now."

"Yeah. And maybe there's really a Santa Claus after all."

"You mean there isn't?" I made a mock pout. "What about *Miracle on Thirty-fourth Street*?"

Jess bopped me with the pillow.

Jesse went to talk to "mommy dearest," and I sat down for some pancakes. Hot—thanks to the microwave. I poured pure maple syrup on the side of the plate and dug my fork into the steaming stack. Mom sat across from me, watching.

Teddy was there, too, feeding his favorite doll. Her face was covered in mashed pancake and syrup oozed down the side of her face, but Mom didn't even notice. She was fidgeting with a napkin, twisting it tighter and tighter.

"Mom," I said in between mouthfuls. "Are you okay?"

"Yeah, baby, I'm okay. I just didn't get enough coffee yet, that's all." She took a slug from her favorite mug. It had flowers blooming all over it. *You'd figure she'd be sick of flowers, but no.*

Then she started pinging on the mug with what was left of her chewed-up nails. She had to use the fronts of her fingers, the nails went so low. Ping, ping, ping, ping.

"Seems like maybe you had too much," I commented.

"No, darling; what I've had too much of is life. Worry when I start pouring vodka in my cup, okay?" She smiled at me sweetly and held her cup up in a mock toast.

"Gee, you don't have to get all cynical," I said, feeling wounded.

"Mommy, what's vodka?" Teddy asked. His doll now had red fruit juice all over her dress; apparently she hadn't been thirsty.

"It's a grown-up drink, honey. But you're not supposed to have it until after lunch."

Teddy shrugged, seeming satisfied. He put his baby doll over his shoulder and burped it. When he took it off, he had sticky syrup globbed all over his shoulder, dripping down Mom's purple beaded vest that he'd "borrowed." But Mom still paid no attention.

"You upset Jesse a little," I said. *And me.*

"Did I?" Mom looked like she had a lot more to say than that, but she glanced at Ted and kept her mouth shut.

"Mommy, I'm gonna give my baby a bath, okay?"

"Okay, sweetie."

Teddy stowed his gooey doll in Mom's favorite hand-bag—he liked to use it as a baby carrier—and sprang out of the room with his bundle of joy. He really *was* in a bouncy mood.

"Uh, Mom? Do you realize you just gave Teddy permission to run the bathtub by himself?"

"What? Oh my God!" She shoved her chair back and rushed out.

I continued to eat; I was incredibly hungry. Mom came

back a few minutes later. "What's Ted up to now?" I asked, chewing like a cow.

"He's reading his baby a book. Thanks. I zoned out there." She pulled a chair by me and sat. "Sam, I'm sorry. I'm really tired. Between Jesse's attack, and then Gwen being here last night, I barely slept, and then you—doing what you did. . . . I guess I did get a little angry about you and Jesse. You *are* my daughter."

"I'm sorry, too. I'm sorry you have to go through so much because of me."

"It's not because of you, baby. You and Jesse got a raw deal, that's all. I just—I just want everything to turn out all right for you." She started to cry.

I hugged her tight. "I love you, Mom."

"I love you, too, baby."

"This is quite the Hallmark moment, isn't it?" We let go and turned to face Gwen. Jesse was right behind her; I tried to gauge what'd happened in the living room by his face, but I couldn't read it. He just looked kind of dazed.

"Yes, Gwen. We like Hallmark moments around here. And I enjoy baking apple pies, too. Do you have a problem with that?" asked Mom.

"Not at all," Gwen said. "I think that's nice."

No one responded to that. It was impossible.

"Well, Jesse, I'll leave you to eat. I'll see you later, yes?"

"Yeah, you'll see us later," he corrected. But his voice didn't carry its usual bite.

"Of course." She gave me and Mom a smile I would've

assumed was fake just the day before; but now I couldn't be sure. And then she pecked Jess on the cheek. When she moved away, I saw he was holding a scroungy blue pillow in the shape of a cat.

Jesse pulled back a chair and dropped into it, also dropping a sandwich bag full of pills on the table. His mom had brought his meds. *Awww* . . . He poured a glass of juice and started popping the pills. The sorry lump of a pillow was on his lap, pressed between him and the table. He kept his eyes focused on the pills.

"Hungry, Jesse?" Mom asked.

He nodded, but he still wouldn't look at her.

"Jesse, don't build a wall between us, okay?"

He shrugged.

Mom reached across the table and put her hand on his. Now he kind of had to look at her if he wanted his hand back. "Normally I wouldn't approve of your relationship with my daughter. I can't lie about it. But circumstances are such that . . . well, let's just say that you kids are reacting to a world gone mad." She squeezed his hand. "Don't be uncomfortable around me, Jesse. I don't want any ill will floating around in the air. I can accept that you two are—together. I hope you can accept me accepting it."

He stared at her numbly, then nodded.

"Just curious then," she added. "Are you ever going to speak to me again?"

He gave her a slight smile. "Yeah. Thanks, Mrs.—uh, Ellen. You're the best, really. I'm just kind of—my mom, um—"

"What happened?" asked Mom.

"And what's that nasty cat thing on your lap?" I asked, more to the point.

Jess gave me a hurt look. "I made 'that nasty cat thing.' In art class, in third grade."

Oops.

"I gave it to my mom for Mother's Day. It's a 'feel better' pillow. It was supposed to make her happy when she was sad. She was always crying after my dad left."

"Your mom cried?" I was shocked. "I don't remember that."

"Yeah, she never did it during the day. In the middle of the night, I'd come into her room and find her like that—" He stopped, pulled the pillow from his lap, and examined it. It was real raggy, but actually not bad for a third grader. There was a decent cat face drawn on it with markers, and a tail glued to its back. It was the stitching that needed help; there were big gaps, and white fluff stuck out between them.

"I guess it worked, kind of. She stopped crying . . . but she didn't get happy. She got—mean." He stared at the cat, mesmerized.

"Jess . . . ," I said softly. I got up, rounded the table, and hugged him. I'd actually never noticed Gwen's relationship with him before his dad left. Maria was always taking care of him when I was around; I didn't know they'd ever shared a tender moment.

I pulled a chair close to him. "So what brought about the second coming of Kitty?" I asked in my usual delicate way.

He laughed a little at that. "She gave him back to me so I'd feel better. She saved him all this time. I never knew . . . " Jesse rested the kitty on the table, folded his arms next to it, and sunk his head into them. I knew he was crying, even though he was trying to be quiet about it.

I rubbed my palm across his back. "That's great, Jess. Your mom has a heart after all. Who'd a-thunk it?"

"Sam!" Mom was appalled at my lack of tact.

But I knew what I was doing. Humor's the best medicine, after all.

It worked. Jesse laughed again, sat up, and swabbed at his eyes.

"Ready to eat?" I asked.

"Yeah."

I got up and took his plate of coldcakes to the microwave, returning a minute and twenty seconds later with a steaming breakfast for him.

"Thanks," he said, giving me his killer smile. It always sent a pang straight to my heart. I picked up Kitty from the table and had a close look.

"You'll never make it as a seamstress, kid," I told Jess.

He smiled again. "Darn."

Chapter 14

The psychologist's office was also on Central Park West, only a few blocks away. But we left an hour early so Jess wouldn't have to feel rushed. We were under orders from Maria to combine the doctor visit with another nice walk for Jesse.

Mom kissed me goodbye. "Sam, don't be nervous. This is good for you."

"Yeah, better go before I take a scissor to my clothes or something, right?"

"Baby, I made the appointment before—today. I just hadn't told you yet. I didn't want you to spend a couple of days being nervous." She looked me up and down. "It seems like only yesterday when you really were my baby."

"I'm still your baby," I said. "Thanks for taking such good care of me." I hugged her big-time.

Jess and I headed down in the elevator. He leaned on the back rail, and I leaned on him.

Dr. Chadwick was a puny-looking old guy with a thin frame, thin grey hair, a thick grey mustache, and thick, square glasses. Thick and thin . . . that was him. He wore a bow tie and a smile. That made me feel better, for like one millisecond. Jess and I held hands across from him in his tan office that contained almost no furniture, other than two brown leather swivel chairs (he'd had to bring in a folding chair for Jess). There was also a midsized bookcase filled mostly with magazines and papers, and a tall, lit floor lamp next to him.

He seemed friendly enough, but I could tell it was going to take a lot of effort relating my life to him. I needed my energy for other things, like actually getting through said life.

He already knew the basics. So now came the tough part, right off the bat: How did I feel?

About? I asked.

You tell me, he said.

How much is it costing to play these head games? I feel like shit, I told him.

Why? He had the nerve to ask.

I told him that if he couldn't figure that one out, maybe he should yank all his fancy degrees and certificates off his wall and chuck them in the trash.

Jess told me to can the attitude. Funny guy, that one. . . . Then he got up, just like he'd promised my mom.

If Dr. Chadwick was alarmed at the prospect of being left alone with his hostile patient, he didn't show it.

"Play nice," Jess told me. He bent to kiss me and I saw the strain in his eyes. He'd been trying so hard to kid with me and keep things light, but those eyes couldn't hide the heaviness inside him. Those eyes told the truth, always. He hobbled out; the door sounded so very loud closing behind him.

"Okay, Sam," said Dr. Chadwick. "Since you insist upon me being direct, tell me how you feel about Jesse's cancer. Beyond 'like shit,' please." He sat tall in his chair— as tall as a puny guy could—and blinked behind the glasses, waiting.

"I feel sad and worried, and scared for Jesse—"

"Yes, but what about for you?"

"For me?"

"Of course you're scared for him, and you want to take care of him. But how do you feel about Sam?"

How do I feel about myself? I squirmed in my seat, made a squeak on the leather with my butt. I'd kind of forgotten how to feel at all. . . . I was numb.

How do I feel . . . How do I feel? I swiveled left, swiveled right. Left, right, left, right. I had to come up with something for this guy.

All of a sudden all this stuff I didn't even know I had inside me burst out. "I feel cheated," I blurted out. "I feel alone sometimes, even though he's there with me." I burst into tears. "And I feel so selfish for thinking of myself."

"You don't deserve to be thought of?"

"I'm not the one who's— No, I guess I don't."

"Doesn't Jesse think of you?"

I saw a box of tissues on his bookcase and headed for them, snatching one. "Yes." I sat back down and blew my nose.

"If you're worthy of him, why aren't you worthy of yourself?"

"It's wrong to worry about me." I got up again. This time I took the whole box back to my seat; it was a tan marble color. He'd bought tissues to match the office. "Jesse's the one suffering."

"Sam, you're suffering, too. You can't hold everything inside. Your mother called me about what happened today."

"Wonderful."

"You're grieving the loss of your father and the potential loss of your boyfriend. You need to let your grief out, willingly or otherwise."

"You see me crying here, don't you, goddamn it?"

"Who are you crying for?"

I stared at him, stricken. That question hurt so much, but I didn't know why. I jumped out of my seat, flung open the door, and ran into Jesse's arms.

"What, what?" he asked, gripping me as I sobbed into his shirt.

"Sam, please come back in," I heard Dr. Chadwick say behind me. I shook my head no. "Jesse, you come, too. We'll tell Mrs. Everfield it was my idea."

I wheezed from the effort of crying. I'd gathered a fistful of Jess's shirt with one hand, and my other one rested on his head. It had a slightly gritty feeling—hair follicles were starting to push their way out. They wouldn't get far; the chemo drugs had cleared out of him, but those doctors were just gonna put him through it again. *And I pushed him to let them.*

"C'mon, Sam. Let's go back in." Jesse's voice was a lullaby.

I released his shirt, got off of him, reached for his hand as he got up.

"Sam," Dr. Chadwick said when we were seated back inside, "you're feeling guilty about the pain you're in. You seem to think that it takes away from Jesse. Can you see that?"

I looked into the lamplight and didn't answer.

"You're caring for him, but you need to take care of yourself, too. It's like when you're on an airplane and they give the emergency instructions. Have you ever paid attention to them?"

Again I said nothing. Jesse took my hand, pressed warmth into it. But still I faced the light.

"They say that when the oxygen masks drop, you have to secure yours first, and then place it on someone needing assistance. You're no good to someone else—someone depending on you—if you don't help yourself."

True, I had to admit.

"If you lose consciousness, what will happen to Jesse?"

I looked at Jess, looked into his beautiful eyes. I so didn't want anything to happen to him.

"But I can't help him anyway—"

"Sam." Now Jess was crying. "You *do* help me. That's what I was trying to say earlier. I couldn't get through this

108

without you. I was lost in my anger; you brought me back."
I didn't know what I'd done with the tissues, so I wiped at
his eyes with my fingers.

"I'm here for you, too. I love you," he said. He kissed
my cheek.

Dr. Chadwick leaned forward in his chair. "The important thing, Sam, is not to deny your emotions. Let the
sorrow out and it'll go. Hold it in, and you'll choke on it."

That was easy to say, just let it out. But I was afraid
I'd be destroyed by what I'd be unleashing.

"I don't know," I said. "I could try, I guess."

"Okay, Sam. That's a good start. And I'm going to help
you help yourself." Dr. Chadwick smiled. He really was an
all right guy, for a shrink. "I just can't do it unless you're
willing. Does that make sense to you?"

"Yeah," I said. I shifted my feet; they kicked against
the tissue box. I picked it up, plucked a tissue, and blew
hard.

We talked a while longer, about how I felt when Jesse
had his treatments, when he was in intense pain, when I was
away from him in school. I answered all kinds of questions
about me. Then the doctor asked me how I saw the future.

I knew the answer, but I wasn't sure I should say it; I
was afraid I'd get committed or something. But then, I did.

I said, "I don't want to live without Jess."

Chapter 15

Dr. Chadwick didn't send for the guys in white coats. He said he wasn't even gonna tell my mom. Our session was confidential, and nobody except Jesse knew. Jess looked a lot more upset than Dr. Chadwick, but he didn't say a word. Dr. Chadwick said we'd cross that bridge if we came to it, and he thanked me for my honesty.

Opening up like that felt pretty good. I felt lighter. Jess, however, looked like he was weighted down with an anvil.

Jess and I held hands when we left. We didn't talk in the elevator or in the lobby, and not even on the sidewalk until we were half a block away. He stopped short just as we reached the corner curb, and pedestrians brushed past on both sides. He pressed his lips against my ear.

"Sam, you've got to knock all this suicide crap out of your head. I've got so much to worry about as it is. . . ."

I didn't say anything, just watched the flashing red words: DON'T WALK. DON'T WALK.

He pulled away now, staring. He took my other hand and squeezed them both. "What about all that stuff you said about me not being gone . . . about me being in your heart?

Was that just BS?" His fingers pressed hard into my hands, just below the point of inflicting pain. I looked away again, at the solid red sign: DON'T WALK. Fine with me; with every step I took, I was avoiding a hidden land mine.

I wanted so badly to rest. To stop walking.

I turned back to Jess—faced the burden in his eyes. "No, of course it wasn't bullshit," I said in a whisper, not afraid of the people passing by hearing me, but of hearing the words myself. *More burden.*

"But you don't want to do it anymore, is that it?" he said. "You're just going to cop out on both of us?"

By now my hands were red from the pressure; numbed.

The sign flashed to green. WALK.

"Sam, promise me you'll stop thinking all this crazy shit." He squeezed into my palms deeper. A throbbing broke through the numbness. "Promise me."

Words teetered at my lips, unwilling to go further, even though I wanted so badly to make Jess feel better. I tried getting them out, tried to make them go. "I—" *How can I swear to something I don't know I can do?* "I promise I'll try, okay?"

He stared into me for what seemed like forever. Finally he nodded slowly, dropping my hands. "I guess." His lips trembled. He looked away now, toward the park. Green leaves shifted back and forth in the wind.

I wiggled my fingers, felt warm sensation creeping back into them. *Is it better to be numb, to feel none of the pain we're in? Would I want to live like that, if I could? Would that be living? Or is it better to just stop walking?*

Jess still stared at the trees. *What is he feeling, really?* I couldn't have a clue, couldn't know what it was like to start treatments over and over, with almost no hope. . . .

Treatments. *Shit!*

It was then that I remembered. Jess's new experimental treatment was starting, and with all that had happened in the past two days, we hadn't even talked about it. I reached for Jess's hands, fit my fingers around his. He looked back at me, his face filled with sorrow and fear.

"You're nervous about tomorrow, aren't you," I said.

Jess was scheduled to go in the next day for the preliminary work on his new stem cell treatment. He was going to be in the hospital for six days. It'd been in my mind, but it got pushed back by what had happened last night.

A lot was riding on that treatment. It wasn't Jesse's "last hope"—the doctors had a bunch of experimental treatments to try—but they'd made it clear it was probably his best hope by far.

Jesse sighed and clutched my hands tightly. "I feel all jittery again, like I'm back to the beginning."

"It'll be okay."

"I hate the hospital. I hate the smell of it. . . ."

"I'll stay with you as much as possible—you know that. And I'll make sure you get a great send-off tonight."

He smiled now. "Who would've thought that a priss like you could degenerate so quickly?"

"You knocked the priss right out of me," I said, leaning against him, enjoying the feel of his heartbeat. I loosened one hand from his and stroked his back. "Let's get a room."

112

"How? We need ID, don't we?" He released my other hand, wrapping his arms around my waist.

"I heard a couple of girls talking about a hotel on Fourteenth near Eighth Avenue that doesn't ask for anything except cash. It was popular on prom night."

"Fourteenth and Eighth?" His warm breath tickled the inside of my ear. "Not the best neighborhood. . . . "

"Not the worst, either," I said, sliding my hand down to his butt and squeezing.

"True." He held me tight, so tight. "Call your mom. Let her know we're going out."

"Mom?" I could barely hear her through the static. I'd never had luck with cells, which was why I rarely used my phone. Jess was sitting on a hydrant, talking to his mom. I paced, trying to find clear airwaves.

"Sam? Where are you?"

"I'm down the block from Dr. Chadwick's."

"How was your session?" I could hardly understand her through the "ssshhh" sound, which didn't stop no matter how much I shifted my position.

"Good." The DON'T WALK sign again flashed red: an endless cycle.

"Really?"

"Really."

"That's wonderful, baby." She didn't press for more and I didn't offer it.

"Listen . . . I just wanted to let you know . . . Jess and

me—we're going out. In case you checked his apartment later and got worried."

The static was enough to make me scream. I marched around the corner, and finally the line was clear. "What did you say, Mom?" It had sounded like "Don't go on a Boeing."

"I said, 'Where are you going?' "

That's what I was afraid she'd said. I paused. "Do you really want to know?" A guy in a suit walking by stopped for a second, thinking I was asking him.

Now she paused. "Sam . . . just come home. I'll give you guys privacy, okay? I don't want you out there, in some seedy dive. . . . "

I imagined my bed creaking away. "Mom, I can't do that. I just can't. We'll be okay."

"I'm not stupid, Sam. The Hilton's not going to let two underage kids check in."

"We'll be fine." There was a squealing of tires, then a car horn honked long and loud.

Mom sighed. "Is this my punishment for writing smut all these years? If I switch to Christian writing, will things be different?"

"Only with your royalty checks."

She laughed. "Amen to that." There was another long pause. "Be careful, baby. I love you."

"Love you, too, Mom."

I went back around the corner; Jess was just hanging up with his mom. A bus roared by with a big ad on its side for ABC's newest hit comedy.

"Your mom okay with it?" he asked, rising from his perch. Grey smoke billowed from the bus's rear in great puffs.

"Sort of. . . . What about yours?"

"I told her we were going to dinner and a movie or something. She asked what time we need to be at the hospital tomorrow. She's coming."

"Huh . . . what do you make of that?"

"I'm thinking maybe there's a bunch of elves slaving away up at the North Pole, and some reindeer taking flight practice, too."

Jess settled his arms around me and nibbled on my ear. *If only Saint Nick could drop ship a miracle our way.*

The hotel's neighborhood leaned more toward the worst than the best. The hotel itself seemed days from closure by building inspectors: chunks were missing from the brick facade, and the rusted fire escape looked none too sturdy. But we were there, we were horny, and we were going in.

As expected, Jesse had no problem renting a room. While he checked in using two bullshit names, I took in what was supposed to be a lobby: a dimly lit narrow hallway with one rickety wooden folding chair. Fly strips were hanging from the ceiling—at least, I guessed that's what they were; they looked like unraveled rolls of film, but flies were stuck to them. The speckled linoleum floor had probably been black and white at some point, but it was now black and brown from the layers of filth caked on it. But the most alarming thing about the place was the desk clerk's distinct resemblance to Norman Bates. I hoped he wouldn't mention his mother.

Jesse finished checking in, the clerk gave me this seriously creepy smile, and we got on the elevator, which barely held the two of us. Not too many people must have checked in with luggage in this place. After a shaky elevator ride that tossed us like salad, we got off on the fourth floor. The lighting in the hallway made the lobby look like Times Square; I would've been scared, but anticipation was the stronger emotion at the moment.

Jess flicked on the light in our room, and I could've sworn things were scampering into corners. The bed was more like a prison cot, the lamp had no shade, and the hotel's HOURLY RATES red neon sign flashed incessantly outside our window.

"Paradise it's not," I told him.

Jess took me in his arms, kissed me, stroked me, and nudged me toward the bed. We fell on it with a squeak of springs and a thud, practically sinking to the floor. The blanket felt rough. The pillows were flat. But we were alone, together.

And Jesse was strong, the strongest he'd ever been with me. He took charge, and it was damn thrilling. What a rush—to be loved with such force.

Where is all this energy coming from?

As if he'd heard my thought, Jesse whispered in my ear, "Tonight, while I can, I want to show you how much I love you."

That boy loved me a lot.

Chapter 16

Jesse was going to be part of a clinical trial, which meant they were going to try an experimental treatment on him and see if it worked. Put like that, it didn't sound too hopeful—Jess being a human guinea pig so the doctors could try some unproven technique. But the proven techniques weren't working for Jess—they'd never worked for anyone with his kind of cancer—and clinical trials were his only hope.

Dr. Raab had found a few he thought had promise, that would give Jesse a chance. He recommended one protocol combining high doses of chemotherapy and total body radiation, followed by a stem cell transplant. He believed that because the treatment was so aggressive and combined these three factors, it was Jesse's best shot.

When Jess first told me about the new treatment, I looked for information about it online. The stem cell transplant at the end of the treatment was supposed to heal the bone marrow destroyed by the large doses of chemo and radiation. The doctors were using Jesse's own stem cells for the transplant, so they had to remove them first. That's what he was going into the hospital for now—they were giving Jesse medicine for five days to increase his stem cell production. Then they'd draw blood and pass it through a machine to remove the cells. Then the stem cells would be treated with drugs to destroy any cancer that might be there. They'd be frozen while Jess underwent the chemo and radiation.

They were keeping him in the hospital for the five days, plus the day they were taking the blood; then he could come home. He had two weeks off, and then for three weeks, he'd go in every three days for his chemo treatments. Once they did the radiation, he'd be back in the hospital for at least three weeks because his immune system would be too weak to be exposed to the outside world.

Jess stopped short in the doorway of his hospital room; I was right behind and banged into him.

"Sorry!" I waited for him to move or at least say something, but he didn't. "Jess?"

"Jesse, what's the matter?" Gwen—the new, compassionate Gwen—said, coming around me.

But he just stood there, his hands gripping the door frame. After a few moments he turned to us.

"I don't think I want to do this."

"*What?*" Gwen and I asked in unison.

"If chemo and radiation are supposed to be helping me, why am I in such worse shape when I'm getting them? Since I've been off treatment, I feel so much better." His eyes were sad, so sad. "I'm going to be worse, aren't I? With higher doses of chemo, I might not be able to walk." I could see he was holding back tears. He hated that damned wheelchair more than anything else. He hadn't needed it in so long. . . .

"You don't know that, Jess. I'm sure—," I began.

"Jesse, you need to do this," Gwen said, cutting me off. "The regular treatments weren't working."

His tears were falling now, and Jesse clung to the door frame like we were going to try and force him into the room.

I hung back, trying to let Gwen do the mom thing, but why didn't she hug him or something? She looked like she wanted to, actually—to hug him. She raised her arms like she was going to, but then just left them in the air, frozen, until she dropped them again. I felt kind of bad for her. It had to suck, being like that. Trapped by the barriers she'd created.

"Jesse, go in," Gwen said. It sounded more like a plea. But he was so wrapped up in himself, I'm not sure he heard her.

"Excuse me, Gwen," I said finally, brushing past her. I couldn't stand watching any longer; at the moment, he needed more than she could give him.

He fell into my arms. "C'mon, Jess. Let's go sit on the bench in the hall." I guided Jess past Gwen, who said nothing.

We headed down the corridor, our feet scuffling the shiny white floor, past the nurses' station, past the gurneys lined up against the wall, around the corner to the long cushioned seat. We kind of plopped down together, and the cushion made a whooshing noise.

"Jess, please do this," I said. "I know it sucks, but please, do it." He was right, the place did smell bad—a sickening combination of Lysol and misery.

"Maybe it's better if I just stop now," Jesse choked out, still leaning on me. "Maybe we could have a few good months, at least."

"That's what this is about, isn't it?" Seeing him in such anguish, I felt like my heart was going to split right open. "It's because of last night. You want to be like you were last night."

Jesse blubbered into my shoulder.

"Dr. Slater to OR three, *stat*. Dr. Slater to OR three, *stat*," an announcement blared.

"Jesse, sweetheart, I don't know what to say, except it just can't be that way right now. But maybe you'll get better. Maybe this treatment will work, and then—"

"I want to make love to you, not just lie there. . . . "

I rubbed his back. "You don't just lie there, Jess. You're incredible—always." God, I hoped Gwen wasn't listening around the corner; then we'd be screwed. Compassionate or not, Gwen wouldn't stand for Jess and me having sex.

He sucked in a breath, blew it out. "I want . . . to be . . . a real man."

"You so are! You don't think I liked it before last night?"

His fingers dug into my sides. "Yeah, but—"

121

"You're willing to throw away the possibility of survival for a few months of great sex?" It was flattering, actually, but I wasn't going to tell him that. "Talk about fucking yourself."

Now I really felt guilty for having suggested that room. Even worse, because knowing what was happening as a result, I wouldn't change a thing. Part of me wanted to grab Jesse's hand and flee with him, far from that scent of sanitized torment, and back to the room that had turned out to be paradise after all. But the desperate need to keep on trying—well, that filled a bigger part of me.

"Look, Jess. We have to stop talking about this for now, okay?" I leaned into his ear. "Your mother's waiting for us. If she decides to eavesdrop around the corner, we're pretty much over and done. Get it?"

"We're pretty much over if I go in there, Sam."

"Only if *you* decide we are." I pushed him off my shoulder and stared into his red eyes. "Jess, you might feel good after it's all over, after the transplant."

"Yeah, sure." He blinked, releasing another tear. "Even if that happens, it'll be after how much time? Time we can't ever get back . . . "

I kissed the tear from his cheek, then looked him in the eyes again. "Hey, you're not going to start the chemo for two weeks, you know."

He shrugged, but something in his eyes softened.

"*And* . . . ," I broke back in, "for the next five days, they're only giving you drugs to make more stem cells. Think about what we can do in your bathroom when I visit." I raised my eyebrows, trying to be funny and suggestive at the same time.

He had to smile. "But what if I have a roommate?"

"He'll need to find his own date," I said.

❄

Gwen looked even more frozen when we got back to the room. She was perched stiffly on the corner of Jess's bed, her black Prada bag beside her, staring at the white wall.

"Mom?" Jess said.

She turned to us and blinked—like she hadn't realized we were there.

"Mom, are you okay?"

"The doctor was here looking for you, Jesse," she said. "I told him to come back in a little while."

"Thanks."

She turned to me, her gaze sharpening. Things falling into focus. "Samantha, shouldn't you be leaving for school?"

"I have a final at noon." I'd had one at nine, too, but it was math and I was failing anyway. I'd decided to complete my dazzling free fall by cementing my fate with the New York State Board of Regents.

"I'm sure you'll do well, having spent last night carousing with Jesse instead of studying," said Gwen. She was real sharp now.

Unfortunately, she had a point.

"Speaking of studying," Jess said. "Mom, would you go to Midland and get me some lessons? I might as well do something while I'm lying around here."

"You mean you're going to start your school work again?"

Jess shrugged. "Yeah, why not? Sam and I can study together over the summer. I mean, I might as well get my diploma, right?"

That was great news.

"That's great news, Jesse," said Gwen.

Swell. Now Gwen and I were sharing thoughts.

Gwen shifted her position on the blanket, recrossing her not-at-all-bad-for-late-forties legs. She wore a short black dress—her usual hospital color.

Jess opened up his suitcase. He took out his pajamas, toiletries, and a notebook, leaving in the rest of his clothes. He flipped the case cover closed, then opened it again, dug under the clothes, and took out his cat pillow. He propped it on the bed covers.

Gwen stared at it.

She got up, stood in front of Jesse, kind of hesitating. Then she put her arms around him, leaned her head against his chest. "I love you, Jesse."

Wow.

He hugged her back, grasping tight.

The look on his face was a little boy's. A third grader who'd just given his mom a kitty pillow he'd made so she'd feel better.

Who would have thought that nine years later, that cat's time would finally come?

"Mom, what are you doing here?" I'd come back from my chemistry final to find my mother at the hospital, sitting with Jesse. He looked dazed—kind of sleeping with his eyes open. "Jess, you okay?" He didn't answer, and he didn't seem to know I was there.

"He's fine, Sam. Don't worry. He just woke up. They had him in the OR, inserting a tube into his chest—I think the nurse said it was called a Hickman line—to take blood from and give him his treatments with." I winced. It sounded painful.

"It didn't hurt him, baby," she said softly. "He was sedated—that's why he's like this now. It's better for him. Now he won't have to get all those injections."

Mom got up. "You sit next to him." She gave me a kiss, moved into the chair facing the bed.

I sat and took Jess's hand. No response—he was all zombied out. But maybe somewhere inside he felt my touch.

I noticed a cookie bouquet on the night table—a vase of cookies on tall sticks in the shapes of happy faces, hearts, and flowers. "Mom. You brought that, didn't you?"

She nodded. "I not only brought it. I baked it."

Mom was so doofy, bless her heart. She said, "You know, when I walked in here, when I saw Jesse lying there unconscious"—she stopped, looking at Jess with this genuine caring, and I loved her even more for that, that she could selflessly feel for the boy who was screwing her daughter—"I realized why you act so irresponsibly about everything else in your life. Being seventeen and in agony over the welfare of someone you love—that's probably the hardest thing you'll ever have to endure." She sighed, crossed her legs. She was wearing slacks instead of her usual sweats. Fancy, for her. "But, Sam, I don't know what to do with you."

"What do you mean, 'do with me'? "

Mom gave me a hard look.

"What? What'd I do?" I asked. "You're not mad about last night, are you?"

"No, Sam. I'm not mad about last night." The words came out slow, each one carefully pronounced. "I'm certainly not thrilled, but I'm not angry."

"Then what is it?" I wished she would just tell me; my nerves were stirring, and I must have passed the feeling through to Jess because he shuddered. Mom and I stopped and watched him, but he was still a space cowboy.

"I went to your school today, to try and arrange for you to have home study over the summer. I told them you were trying so hard, but the problem was that you just couldn't concentrate in school with Jesse in his condition. Do you know what they said?"

I had an idea. . . .

Her voice was rising like an airplane on takeoff. "They said if you were trying so hard, how come you didn't show up for your math regents?"

Bingo! "But I was already failing—"

"*Samantha!*" That was the sharpest my mom had ever said my name. It made my soul cringe. "I never want to hear about you doing anything like that from anyone but you again. If you're going to act like a fool, don't make *me* look like one, too. Have the courtesy to inform me *beforehand*. And then I'll know not to try and help you anymore."

Now that is sad. It made me feel just awful. My mom was ready to give up on me. I wiped my eyes with my free hand.

"Don't cry, Sam," said Mom, in a tone still angry, but not biting. "I said *next time* I'd know not to help you. I didn't say I wouldn't help you now." She reached into her tote bag and pulled out a bunch of textbooks. "I had to speak to each of your teachers, the dean, and the headmaster, but I got permission for you to work at home. You can also home-study in the fall."

"Mom . . ." I was touched. I let go of Jess's hand so I could run over and hug her. "Thanks."

She clenched her fingers into the hollow of my back. "Sam, please take this seriously. You're the only one who can truly help you."

"I will, Mom." I meant it, too.

When I sat down again Jess smiled. "Sam! You're back!" he exclaimed, all slurry. He reached out and I took his hand. "Ready to head into the bathroom?" He gave me a drunken wink.

I felt Mom's heated stare on me. "Shhh, Jess. My mom's here."

"She is?" He looked around. It took him a moment to spot her in front of him. "Hi, Ellen!"

127

I wanted to evaporate or something. "Sorry, Mom," I told her. "I—I had to promise him. Uh, it was the only way I could get him to start his treatment."

"You enticed him into his hospital bed by offering sexual favors?"

I nodded.

She let out a long, low whistle. "I should never have let you read my books."

Chapter 17

We never did make it into the bathroom that day. Mom left to pick up Teddy, but Jess was way too woozy. Thank God, because then Gwen came in with deli food for Jess, so he wouldn't have to eat the hospital slop. She brought him egg salad with extra mayo on a pumpernickel bagel with tomato, a Caesar salad, ginger ale, and rice pudding. Jess needed extra calories so he wouldn't lose too much weight.

Jess wasn't that hungry. He took like, two bites of the sandwich, and I think he only did that to show Gwen he appreciated her effort. I hadn't given food a thought all day, and seeing it set those salivary glands in motion. Like a human garbage disposal, I practically slid that salad down my throat without chewing. The bagel was more of a challenge.

"Rice pudding?" Jess asked, after I'd scarfed down everything else.

Hmm . . . creamy pudding. Tempting, but I felt Gwen's heavy stare, and suddenly I felt like I'd snatched the food out of Jess's mouth. "Save it for later. You might get hungry," I told him, even though I *did* want it.

I eyed Jess's cookie bouquet. *Yum*. I took a heart, pulled off the clear wrap, and bit a chunk.

The nurse came in and gave Jess his medicine—right in the tube in his chest. I couldn't bring myself to look directly at it. I just hated the thought of a tube jammed into him—it made me ill.

"Does . . . does it hurt you?" I asked him when the nurse left, keeping my eyes on his face.

"No. I'm just a little achy all around it. They told me that'd pass." He smiled. "I'm all right, Sam." He buttoned his red pajama top again. "I can take showers, do *whatever* I want." He gave me a knowing look. It was the perfect combination of suggestion for me and ambiguity for Gwen.

I didn't dare look at her, though. I'm no good at covert operations.

I bit off another piece of cookie heart, crunching it in my mouth.

Gwen sighed. "Well, it's getting late. I'm going to go. Samantha?"

I guessed she was offering to share a cab, and I guessed it made sense, except I didn't want to go yet. I didn't want to go at all.

"I'm gonna hang out awhile," I told her. After a second I added, "But thanks."

She shrugged, stood, and gave Jess a quick kiss and a hug, which he returned. I was glad for him.

Then the door slid shut with a "shoosh" sound, like someone whispering "quiet" to us. It felt that way in there, sitting next to Jess with that tube in his chest, helpless and soon alone—it felt like we'd been shooshed into uneasy silence. I set the gnawed remains of Jess's heart cookie down on the swivel table and felt sick.

But Jess didn't share my discomfort. He had something else on his mind, looking from me to the bathroom, then back to me, and then the bathroom. Real subtle, this guy of mine.

"Jess, we have like twenty minutes before I get the heave-ho."

He made a sad face—pretty phony, but with a little truth to it.

"Jess, I don't have a final until twelve tomorrow. I'll come first thing, okay?"

He smiled. "Okay, then I'll come."

"You are the biggest perv!"

"Yeah, right. And who was it that suggested the bathroom in the first place?"

"I'm just glad you *don't* have a roommate," I said. "Our luck, he'd have a big mouth and a bad bladder."

Jess laughed, then patted the mattress. "C'mere." He reached down and lowered the bar. "See how it's done?"

"Three's a crowd," I said, pointing to his kitty pillow grinning up at me from beside him.

He chucked it to the end of the bed. I slid in next to him, between the white cotton sheets, and into his arms. We kissed, kind of awkwardly because I was trying to stay away from his chest.

"It's okay, Sam," he said. "Touch me."

I leaned into him, still feeling kind of nauseous. I had to remember to eat regular meals; it was one of those functioning details of life that were so hard to focus on right now.

We made out, with a little petting thrown in for good measure—the kind of stuff we'd be working our way up to if we'd started dating the normal way.

If we'd started dating . . .

If all the bad hadn't happened, would Jess be all over me right now at a movie, or Cindy Evans?

Why was that in my mind?

Ding, ding, ding. "Your attention, please. Visiting hours are now over. Please make your way to the nearest exit. Thank you."

I started to get up, but Jess held me back, giving me one last consuming kiss.

"First thing, right?" he asked, looking lonely already.

"First thing," I agreed.

God, I wished I didn't have to turn my back on those sad eyes.

Ding, ding, ding. "Visiting hours are now over. Visiting hours are now over. Please make your way to the nearest exit at once."

I stopped at the door, went back for one more last kiss. "Sleep well."

"Not likely."

I headed out the door, swiping at my tears. This sucked, walking away.

I cried all the way home in the cab. I pictured myself in that bed with Jess, snuggling under the blanket—holding him, touching him, smelling him. Then suddenly I wasn't

there with him. Cindy was. And that brought on a whole
new round of tears.

Ding! The elevator door slid open and I stepped into
Oz again.

My life seemed punctuated by bells—first at the hospital, and now here. A reminder of time running out, like the
grains of sand pouring through the Wicked Witch of the
West's giant hourglass. I stood on the yellow brick carpet,
frozen with that thought. My eyes wandered up, up to the
white ceiling to avoid the green lines on the walls. And
there it was, spelled out above me. A message in black, billowy letters, as though the witch had just left the scene:
SURRENDER DOROTHY.

The hallway spun, turbulent and sudden, like life.

Whirling, twirling.

I ran to the wall, swiped at the emerald to try and stay
up. But how could I, how could anyone stand in a world
that at any moment just sweeps you up and hurls you aside?

Dizzy, so dizzy . . . My fingers skidded down, down
the rough green stripes . . . I fell with them.

How could I fight? How could I win? There's no winning when there's no rules. Why was everything so fragile,
so hinged on chance? Or on nothing at all . . . ?

I curled up on the golden rug and squeezed my eyes
shut. But I kept seeing those words swirling, circling in my
mind: SURRENDER DOROTHY. SURRENDER DOROTHY.

Surrender to what? Was the message from the wicked witch, or from the wizard?

That dumb wizard was a fraud, and that goody-two-shoes witch Glenda was useless, with her bad advice and false optimism. The only one you could count on was the wicked witch—she alone was as good as her word.

What was I supposed to do with that?

Stupid hallway. Stupid Glenda, acting like wishes could come true if you worked hard enough for them. Stupid sham wizard, pretending to produce happy endings. Stupid me, for believing in wishes and happy endings, for begging for them still.

I felt wetness on my cheeks, pressed my fingers against my lids hard. I didn't want to cry in Oz. I didn't want to surrender, not really.

For a second I could swear I felt a touch on my head. A warm palm on my crown, giving comfort. Like my dad used to do. . . . Further proof that I was mad.

And if it *was* him . . . if he was some spirit reaching out from the grave . . . what good was that? What good was having him for a moment, then losing him again?

God, it was unbearable.

Ding. Another bell. But it was far . . . so far away this time. And I didn't know whether that was good or bad. I only knew that I was sick of not knowing anything.

And then my mind went black.

Chapter 18

"Sam?"

I came out of the cold black to warmth. A warm body was holding me, pressed against me—a guy. I could tell by the sound of his breathing, and the strength of his arms.

Not Jess. He didn't smell like Jess, or feel like Jess. And I wasn't comfortable like I was with Jess. Still, I was somewhat comforted.

"Sam, are you okay?" I recognized the voice now: Pete.

"What are you doing here?" I asked, somewhat muffled by his shirt.

He pulled away gently, still supporting me gingerly, and stared. He had soft blue eyes that always seemed to be smiling, no matter what the rest of his face was doing. I'd noticed that before, but I always chose to concentrate on the rest of his face, which never looked happy to see me. I was annoying, unable to take a hint, hanging around even though I was the only girl in the crowd. At that moment, I saw it from his point of view and I felt a pang of regret that I'd denied the boys their time alone.

"What am *I* doing here?" His eyes widened and seemed to smile even more. "What are *you* doing balled up out here on the floor?" His hair was scruffy blond, and he wore a baseball cap backward over it, like he almost always did. There were a few stray hairs poking through the back hole in the cap. I loosened myself from his grip and found myself pushing at those hairs, trying to smooth them down. No use.

"I—I guess I had a bad moment," I answered. A slight understatement.

"Yeah," he said, like I'd come up with an explanation that made any sense at all. "Listen, you think . . . you think I could come in and see Jess? Is his mood any better?"

Poor Pete. He just kept trying—a good friend.

I shook my head no. "I'm sorry, Pete, but he's not here. He's in the hospital. . . . "

"Is he okay?"

"Yeah, yeah. He's just starting a new treatment."

Pete let out a heavy, hot breath. I felt the worry in it as it hit me in the face. "Pete . . . I'll talk to him again. I'll get him to see you."

"You think you can?"

I didn't know why, but I really thought I could just then, and I told him so.

Then I heard my apartment door open. For a second I worried that it was Teddy. I didn't want him to see me like this; he'd been so messed with already. But then I realized that it was way past his bedtime.

"Sam?" It was Mom. "Baby, what's wrong?"

Ha. What a question.

Pete moved to make room for Mom, who folded herself around me. "I'm fine, Mom. I just . . . tripped. That's
all." I looked at Pete, who thankfully took the hint and nodded in agreement.

"Pete was just helping me up. He came to see Jess—
he didn't know Jess wasn't here."

"Sam." Mom knew I didn't trip, but she didn't say anything else. What else was there to say? Instead, she played
with a strand of my hair, twisting it in her finger. She studied me, like she was trying to see inside my mind. Even
bloodshot, her eyes were still so loving. Looking into them
always used to make me feel safe, secure—back when I still
believed in fairy tales.

"I'm fine. Really, Mom." She helped me up and I tried
looking away from the stripes as I rose, but they were
everywhere, damn it—an emerald prison.

"Pete, would you like to come in?" Mom knew Pete.
She knew most of Jess's friends.

Pete hesitated, then shook his head no.

"Are you sure? I've got fresh-baked brownies, with and
without walnuts. . . . "

"C'mon Pete. I don't wanna wind up eating all those
brownies myself," I said. Having someone to talk to—
someone who knew Jess like I did—would be awesome.

He looked at me for a second. Then his face matched
his eyes. "Thanks," he said in his husky voice; he was that
kind of guy. Husky—not in size—but in quality. Raw,
ragged—like he was still under construction or something.

Jess always had it together; Pete always looked like he
was coming apart.

Mom left us alone in the kitchen. We ate brownies and talked, me telling him about the last few months, him letting out a lot of his pent-up feelings. I felt so close to him that I told him about me and Jess, that we were a couple. He said he was happy for us. And when he left, after midnight, it was with the promise that I'd talk to Jess in the morning about letting him visit.

I felt better, or at least I thought I did, until I burst into tears again halfway back down the hall from locking the door behind Pete. Mom followed me into my room and sat with me on my bed.

"What's wrong, Sam?"

I didn't answer her. All I could focus on was that Mom's "What's wrongs" were getting terser. And she didn't call me "baby." That made me cry more.

"Sam, when's your next appointment with Dr. Chadwick?"

"Monday," I blubbered.

"Maybe I'll try to get you in tomorrow."

"Nooo . . . " I fell into my pillow, aching inside. I didn't want to leave Jess to go to the shrink, even if I *had* felt good after the first session.

"Sam—oh, forget it." She got up.

"Mom," I moaned. "You're just going to leave me like this?"

"Sam, you're not telling me the problem. There's nothing I can do for you."

"Don't you love me anymore?"

"What kind of a crazy question is that?" She sat back down, hugged me. "Of course I love you, baby."

Ahhh . . . I was "baby" again. My body relaxed a little.

"Sam, what happened tonight? In the hall?"

What had *happened in the hall?* I took a deep breath and blew it out. Mom held me with one arm and stroked my hair with her free hand.

"I'm not sure, exactly. . . . I just keep having all these thoughts about how Jess is only with me because of the cancer, otherwise he'd be with Cindy—he was going to ask her out again, right before he got sick. . . ." I took another breath, thought I was done, but I wasn't. "And then I think about how selfish I am for thinking these things, and how I don't even deserve him. Because I'm grateful to be with him, so that means I must be glad that he's sick. . . . " Tears slicked steadily down my face like rain on a windshield. "And then it all hits me again, how meaningless all of this is, that we can try and try to get by, to be happy. But then in a flash, in one line of a play, it all collapses around us."

I stopped, unable to continue without completely choking on everything that had collected in my throat.

Mom stroked my hair and back, and I burrowed my head into the hollow of her neck, still crying silently. For a while there was no sound except the alternating beats of our hearts. Then she spoke.

"Baby, there's no easy way to come to terms with life, to understand why bad comes with good, why horrible things happen to us. But somehow we have to make our peace, if not with life, at least with ourselves. That's the only part that we do have any control over—our own hearts." She gave me a squeeze. "Unfortunately, instead of loving ourselves and comforting ourselves, we tend to fill up with guilt and sorrow."

I cleared my throat, swallowed some snot. "So how am I supposed to find this peace?"

"Believe in Jesse's love, Sam. Don't beat yourself over the head with what if's. He loves you, and you can hold on to that love while you learn to love yourself."

I sniffed loud in an attempt to suck some air through my clogged nostrils. My eyes were sore and it hurt to hold them open.

"How do you know Jess loves me?"

"I can see it. Anyone can. I'm sure even Gwen has an idea."

"But does he *love* me, or just love me?"

Mom pulled me off her shoulder and looked into my squinting, aching eyes; she looked blurry. "He loves you, Sam. He's in love with you, all right. He's absolutely head over heels mad about you." She hugged me hard. "And if you don't believe me, ask him."

They say you can smell trouble; I always thought it was one of those sayings you don't take literally, but I found out otherwise the next morning. I was all set to talk to Jess and settle my nerves, and to find that peace Mom was talking about. But when I swooshed open Jess's hospital room door, it hit me: a staggering dose of designer perfume—a witch's brew of florals, fruits, and spices combined into an overdramatic and sickeningly syrupy scent. It was a big 'ole wallop of trouble, because I knew who wore that scent, and it felt like my worst fears were sucker punching me.

Somehow I made it past the door and inside. "Sam!" Jess smiled at me, and I tried to focus on him instead of the person sitting next to him, *in my chair*.

Tried, but failed.

There sat Cindy Evans, Miss Friggin' Perfect, from the symmetrical ringlets in her silky auburn hair, right down to her bright, bubble-gum-pink polished pedicure that protruded from her equally electric pink sandals. Cindy always matched—and in every conceivable way.

Damn that Pete. He must have told her Jess was in the hospital. Real nice, after I gave him brownies and everything.

"Okay if I come in?" I asked, then mentally slapped myself. *Why would I ask such a thing? How insecure can I get?* Unfortunately, I kind of knew the answer to that one.

"Yeah. Of course," Jess answered, puzzled.

Cindy gave me one of her BS smiles, curving her pink lips and showing every single one of her sparkling teeth. I went around Cindy—who didn't move—to kiss Jess hello. Then I parked myself there on the bed next to him, coming between them, kind of like I was claiming my turf. Jess didn't say anything, but he stiffened a little.

There was a silence in the room now. Then Cindy craned past me to get a better look at Jess. "You seem to be feeling better," she said.

"Yeah, I am—for now anyway," Jess answered.

"Maybe we could get a bite sometime, when they spring you—"

"No," I interrupted, before I could stop myself. I couldn't believe what a jealous ass I was being, and Cindy just stared at me.

"Umm . . . as I was starting to tell you before she walked in. . . ." Jess looked around me at Cindy. I couldn't catch his eye, which probably was just as well. "Sam and I are together now."

"I see." But she didn't look like she saw at all; she looked like she was ready to pounce in that miniskirt, which left practically nothing to the imagination. "But when we were dating, you did things with Sam all the time. Are you not allowed to do things with other friends now?"

Bitch. Bitch. Bitch. Like she wants to be his "friend." Then again, had I wanted to be just his "friend"? Swell, I was turning on myself. Thankfully I kept my mouth shut.

Jess said, "I can do what I want, Cindy. But right now I want to spend my time with Sam." *Aww.*

Cindy shrugged, like it was no big deal. "I'd better get going. I'll pop by again, now that you're feeling more hospitable. Is that okay?"

"Yeah, sure," Jess answered.

Why, why is he letting her come back? Oh for God's sake, what did I want to do, lock him in a room for myself? It was good, if he wanted visitors. Healthy. But why did *she* have to be one of them—the first one?

Cindy got up and leaned over me to kiss Jess goodbye. I should've gotten up to make it easier, but I didn't. Leaning on my leg, she managed a peck; then she moved back, said goodbye to me coldly, and sashayed her little butt out of the room.

Swoosh went the door behind her; we were in silence again, and this time the awkwardness was mutual.

I wanted to tell him I was sorry about all that, and I wanted to explain that I knew I was wrong. And I wanted to have a conversation to clear the air once and for all about Cindy—I wanted to do all that, but my lips wanted no part of it. They simply refused to open.

We sat next to each other, so close yet not touching, staring at anything not to look at each other, until I had to leave for my final.

Good work, I told myself as I headed down the corridor toward the door. Jess's mouth had barely moved when I kissed him goodbye.

I didn't need Cindy Evans to sabotage us. It was clear that I could do that all by myself.

Chapter 19

Of course, I did brilliantly on my French final—not.

Hey, I was distracted. Every verb came into my head with a picture of Cindy, pretty in pink from head to toe, demonstrating the action.

C'est la vie.

Afterward, I went into the school courtyard. Maybe some fresh air would help me concentrate on my next final—English, Mom's favorite. I really didn't want to let her down again.

There were only a handful of students out there; most went home between tests, or to Grimalda's, the pizza place down the block. But I knew if I left, I might not come back.

I spotted Pete under the big oak tree. He was alone, staring out at the bricks, with his Midland baseball cap backward on his head and a brown paper-covered textbook in his lap. I came closer but he didn't see me, and he didn't break his stare. I cleared my throat to let him know I was there.

He turned, startled. "Oh, hi, Sam."

I stared, wanting to say something pissy about him

telling Cindy that Jess was in the hospital, but I didn't feel comfortable enough to do it.

"What's up?" he asked.

Still I just stood there and said nothing.

"Wanna sit?" he asked, patting the grass next to him. He seemed to accept any strange behavior I exhibited, which made it hard to chew him out.

I sat down, leaning back into prickly bark. My fingers smoothed through cool grass strands.

He turned back to the bricks he'd been staring at, a section of wall holding the Ewing Wing together, where my English final was going to be. I admired those bricks in their simplicity and strength. They were blocks with one purpose, and nothing to stop them from it. A wing, a wall—they were so easy to build. All you needed was a bucket of cement and bricks. A wall was simpler than a wing: there was nothing but a facade. You could wait behind it, just hang out and know you'd be safe. You could stop worrying and know.

"You told Cindy where Jess was." The words came now, backed by the weight of the bricks.

He turned to me. "Yeah, I called her. How'd you know?"

"She was there this morning, with Jess. When I got there."

"Huh," he said, turning back to the bricks.

I grabbed his arm, squeezed into the flesh below his T-shirt sleeve. "Ow!" He pulled away. "What's wrong with you?"

Now there's the question. I knew I could get him to ask

145

it, that he wouldn't always accept my behavior unconditionally.

"All you have to say for yourself is 'huh'?"

"What do you want me to say?"

Why'd you tell her? . . . "I thought—you said you
were glad Jess and I were together. . . ." I looked away, trying to hold back the tears that were always on call, always
ready to deploy at a moment's notice.

"Sam . . . I—" His fingers brushed my face, so soothing. "I *am* glad about you and Jess. I always knew you guys
belonged together. It made me angry, that he didn't see."

I forced a look into his glassy eyes. They were like a
shimmery pond. Maybe that was the problem—that I was
afraid I'd glimpse my reflection in them.

"See what?" I asked.

"That you loved him."

"You knew?"

"Yeah." He let out a little laugh. "I knew."

"Then why'd you tell Cindy?"

"What's the problem with telling Cindy? You shouldn't
be jealous of her."

"Who said I'm jealous?" He gave me an "oh, please"
look and I had to laugh. "Okay, I'm jealous. But she's so
perfect."

"Perfect on the outside should be a warning sign," he
broke in. "No one's perfect, and trying to look it to the
world means there's a whole lot of imperfect inside."

"Huh," I said.

"Is that all you've got to say?" He laughed again. He
had a nice laugh—natural, contagious. I laughed, too.

"Sam, I told her because she's worried about Jesse. We're all worried—all the friends he shut out. I called a lot of people last night—not to have them come rushing over, but just to give them an update. I'm sorry if that bothers you."

"It doesn't. I'm glad Jess has so many friends. It's just . . . *her*."

He smiled. "You know, I bet she always said the same thing about you."

Pete and I talked for a while; then I realized I was nearly late for my English Regents. I rushed into the Ewing Wing entrance, raced down the marble hall, and got in just when they were opening the test booklets.

Eighteen sets of eyes looked up at me, some amused, some curious, some glaring.

I sat at my desk in the left rear corner, flipped opened the test, and pressed the point of my pencil on to the cover of the blue answer booklet.

I filled in my name. I moved the point down a line, pressed, and was about to fill in the date, but I couldn't— I just couldn't. Something inside went *snap!* And my internal mechanisms shut down.

I sat like that, unmoving and broken, pencil poised, the whole time. Then, at the fifteen-minute warning, I felt some stirrings inside and I knew I'd be all right again, that I'd come around.

When the tests were collected, I stowed my pencil and got up like nothing was ever wrong. At least I didn't get a zero; I heard you get points just for writing your name. But I hadn't even put down the date. Did that matter?

I went home and gave Mom the good news about my test. I figured, why wait for the report card? She was okay about it, and took it all in without comment. After last night, I guess she was being careful about what she said. I told her maybe I wouldn't mind talking to Dr. Chadwick early after all. She got me an emergency session, so off I went.

"So Sam, what do you think prompted your anxiety?" Dr. Chadwick asked.

I'd just told him about my collapse in the hall last night, and about thinking my mom and Jess didn't love me—and about being jealous of Cindy, and feeling so helpless about the crazy thoughts I was thinking. And finally, I'd told him about the test.

"You know, Dr. Chadwick, I was hoping you could tell me. Isn't that kind of your job?"

"My job is to help *you* realize why you felt that way."

"I could ask myself the same questions. Why do I need you, if you're not gonna give me the answers?"

Dr. Chadwick laughed. "Unfortunately, Sam, I don't *know* the answers. We have to unearth them together."

I rolled my eyes. This guy was talking excavations. "So maybe I need an archaeologist or something."

He laughed again. "Let's stick to the problem at hand, and dispense with the humor, shall we?"

I shrugged, kicked at the box of tissues I'd stowed at my feet, just in case.

"Now, did anything happen to make you feel unloved?"

I spun in my swivel chair two times, thinking. "My mom didn't call me 'baby.' She always calls me 'baby,' but she didn't last night. And she's been getting snippier and snippier, and I'm afraid"—I could feel the tears coming—"I'm afraid that she's just gonna get fed up with me."

"And what will happen then? Do you think your mother will throw you out into the street?"

"No. I'm just—I want her to like me." The waterworks were open for business now. I snatched a tissue and swiped it across my face. "I guess I know she loves me, but I want her to like me." *Wow—it feels good, saying that. Letting it out.*

"So you think your recent behavior will make her dislike you?"

I nodded.

"Do you think, Sam, that the real problem is you're afraid that *you* don't like you?"

That's what Mom had said last night, kind of. She'd said I needed to learn to love myself. Tears streamed down my cheeks.

"I'm a big fuckup," I said. "And I can't . . . control"—that word really fought to stay put inside—"I can't control anything."

"Who can?" asked Dr. Chadwick.

"No one, I guess." I coughed up a hunk of snot from my throat and spit it into my tissue. "No one can. That's just it—that's it exactly." I stopped to snort out more phlegm. "Mom says I have to find peace with myself."

Dr. Chadwick smiled. "Your mother's a smart woman, Sam." He uncrossed his legs and crossed them the other way. His dark blue sock peeked out between shoe and pants. It was just short of black.

"I think, Sam, that there're two issues at work here. First, you're losing your self-respect because you're shirking your responsibilities. There's an easy way to remedy that: make up the work this summer. Do you agree?"

I nodded.

"And then there's the more complicated issue of wanting to take control of your life and of Jesse's condition. There's the whole feeling of helplessness, and questioning Jesse's love is most likely a by-product of that. You're questioning his emotions because you're up in the air about everything else. Your subconscious is working to protect you. It's saying, 'Better not get too hopeful about this, because everything else has come crashing down.' You'll have to override it."

"How am I supposed to do that?"

"I'm going to teach you a technique to reprogram your subconscious, to make it learn to trust good feelings and happiness. When you come in on Saturday, we'll work on it. I want you to read this information first." He got up and handed me a booklet called "How to Tap."

"You want me to tap dance?"

He laughed again. "No, Sam. Though go ahead if

you'd like to. But this tapping is done with your fingers. You tap them on different points on your arms, hands, and face, and recite what it is you wish to change in your life. It's called EFT, for Emotional Freedom Technique."

I didn't know what to say. If it wasn't a shrink telling me this, I'd say it was off the wall. Hell, it was off the wall anyway.

"Are you serious?" I asked him.

"I am," he said. "And I want you to listen to a CD also, to boost your self-confidence, give you a more positive outlook and to help with total mind and body healing."

"What is it, a lecture?"

"No, Sam, it's subliminal. It just sounds like soothing ocean waves."

I shrugged again. I did a lot of shrugging at $150 an hour, or whatever it was he charged. "Okay. Can I play it for Jess, too?"

"Sure." He got the CD off his desk and handed it to me. "Sam, I'm not going to say some trite cliche, like, 'It's always darkest before the dawn,' or 'When the going gets tough, the tough get going.' " He knelt by my chair and looked into my eyes. "I know life stinks for you right now. But if you want to help yourself feel better, you can. It's really up to *you*."

There sure was a lot riding on me. *Me*—the one who was reading smoky messages on the ceiling and catching glimpses of my dead father—not that I'd ever shared these little tidbits with Dr. Chadwick. All this was riding on the *me* who'd gone from honors English to not getting past filling out her name on the Regents. Me, the girl who was feeling threatened by a girl who dressed like a gumball. This was who I had to rely on: me.

What about Superman? Wasn't he available to swoop in the window with his red cape and boots and make things right?

But there weren't any superheroes.

There weren't even any wizards.

The sham who called himself the Wizard of Oz was probably hiding in a broom closet in the Emerald City outside my apartment, quivering in shame.

Maybe I could join him in there.

Chapter **20**

It was a quarter to seven by the time I got back to the hospital. I should've called to let Jess know I'd be late, but part of me was afraid he'd say to not bother coming.

"Hey, you." Jess smiled at me from his bed. He'd missed me. How could I have doubted that he would? Did I think one stupid Cindy incident would ruin everything?

Yeah, I did.

Jess closed the notebook he'd been writing in, hooked the pen on the cover, and put it on the nightstand. "Feel better now that you're all shrunk up?"

"How'd you know?"

"I called your mom to see where you were. I got worried." I was still standing near the door. He patted the spot beside him on the bed. "Will you come over here? You weren't so shy this morning."

"I—I—Jess, I'm so sorry. . . ." I turned away from him as the deluge began.

"Sam, I was just teasing. Come on . . . please?"

I swiped my face with my arm and shook my head no.

"Sam." The word was soft, next to me. Then Jess's

153

arms were around me, holding me tight. Why wasn't that enough for me to feel safe? "I love you, Sam," he said.

"I love you, too."

He held me while I cried. He said nothing, just held space for me. He was in the hospital with cancer, and he was holding space for me.

My tears stopped after a while. I lifted my face from Jess's soaked hospital gown and looked at him. "I really am sorry, Jess." I wanted to say more, but I was so, so exhausted. "Can we lie down?"

"Sure." We moved to the bed, locked arms around each other, and kissed.

"Sam," he said when we'd stopped, "I love you with every molecule I'm made of. I don't know what else to say to make you feel more secure. Please don't be jealous of Cindy."

"It's just . . . if you hadn't gotten sick, you'd be dating her right now."

"No. I'd be dating you," he said. "I swear, Sam, I would. I think, on some level, we were in love from when we were little. We belong together. We would've found our way." He kissed me on the cheek. "It might have taken me a while to catch on, but we would've found our way."

I was about to agree when the dinging came on. "Visiting hours are now over. . . ."

"Crap," Jess said with a mock pout. "I guess I miss out on the bathroom again."

"There's a lock in there, right?" I asked.

"Yeah."

"Then let's go." I climbed out of bed and he followed. "They can kick me out when we're done."

"'Atta girl, Cindy. Oops, I mean Sam."

I swirled around and glared.

He winked.

He was darn lucky he was so cute.

The next day I finished my final at noon, so I spent the whole rest of the day with Jess.

He looked really happy when I walked in, and not just to see me.

"Guess what?" he asked.

I shrugged. *I hate guessing what. Why can't people just tell you?*

"Dr. Raab is gonna give me medicine so I don't get sick from the chemo! Can you believe it? He said I should have told him before, that I was heaving so much." He looked so, so thrilled, and I was, too.

"That's super, Jess," I said, hugging him. I curled up next to him, tired from the test taking. Today was social studies; I was pretty sure I'd done okay on this one. Trouble was, my idea of okay had taken a slide lately.

Jess asked what was new, and I told him I'd seen Pete twice, and that he really wanted to visit. Jess said sure. It really was fantastic, his being open to seeing people again, even if that did include preciously pink people.

Then Jess asked how my finals had gone. I said I was

reasonably sure I'd passed today's test, but I'd done badly on the French final, and had messed up royally on the English Regents.

"It's all right." He shifted my hair and sucked on my neck. He really knew how to relieve stress. He whispered into my ear, "We'll study all summer, okay?" The words tickled my eardrum. "I'm gonna make sure you don't have to repeat eleventh grade."

"I'll have to keep my distance, or we'll never get anything done," I said as his hands groped all over my T-shirt.

"I missed you, Sam—I missed you last night."

"Hey, I recall you having your way with me before I left—"

"Yeah." He nuzzled against my face. "But as glorious as that was, it didn't make up for being alone last night, and again tonight. . . . "

"I'm sorry, Jess." My gaze hit upon Kitty at the end of the bed. She seemed to be giving me the evil eye.

"Hey, I'm not trying to make you feel bad. I'm trying to make you feel appreciated." He returned his attentions to my neck.

"It's okay, Jess. I know you love me. I went into emotional overdrive or something, that's all." I turned away from the cat and looked toward Jesse's cookie bouquet instead. He hadn't eaten any. I snagged out a smiley face, unwrapped it, and bit off a chunk of where his chin would be. It was passive aggression—poor guy couldn't fight back.

"Did Dr. Chadwick help?"

"Yeah." I opened my backpack, showed him the booklet. "He gave me this to read. He's teaching me tapping on Saturday, to positively reprogram my subconscious."

"Interesting . . . " He looked and sounded skeptical.

"I know—I have my doubts, too. But let's go with it, for now. And he gave me a subliminal CD: ocean waves. I brought my player so we could listen together." I dug out the player and CD, then hit Play. The ocean waters thundered and roared.

"Hmm . . . kind of relaxing," said Jess.

"Think so?" I listened, feeling tenser and tenser. "It makes me feel like I'm drowning," I said. "Like my head's slipping under the foamy waves, going down, down, down."

Jess turned the volume real low. "I don't think you have to pay attention for it to work," he told me. "Especially if it's having adverse effects."

"So how was your day?" I asked, crunching; I'd eaten the smile off smiley's face.

"Same 'ole. Meds go in, blood comes out. They're already testing it for an increase in stem cell production."

"Are you feeling stem celly?"

"Oh, yeah. I'm just brimming with them." The bed creaked as he shifted his position, stretching out his legs. He winced a little.

"You're not in any pain, are you?"

"Not really. Not more than usual, anyway. I'm used to it."

I put the cookie down and touched his shoulders, rubbing them. "Jess, they can increase your medicine dose. You don't have to suffer." I'd been researching pain management on the Web.

"I don't want to be some druggie, flying high." His face was stony now. "Or to veg out into nowhere land. What's the point of living if you're not aware of it?"

I knew better than to argue; he needed to make some decisions on his own. "Lie down, Jess. I'll give you a massage." It said on the National Cancer Institute website that massage was recommended to relieve cancer pain. After reading that, I'd looked up massage techniques.

He must have been hurting, because he lay down without comment or protest—just a small groan as he turned over.

I worked on him for a while, massaging and loosening up his muscles. I ran a nonstop, one-way conversation the whole time. Jess didn't say anything, and I figured he was getting into the massage. As it turned out, he'd fallen asleep.

I stared at his notebook on the nightstand. I knew I shouldn't, but I had to look—I just had to. Amazingly, it was filled with poetry. I was surprised and intrigued, and read page after page.

He'd scrawled angry poems, lashing out at cancer, tumor, treatment, pain. And reflective poems, about the flow of life and death and other meditations. I didn't know Jess wrote poetry.

There were a couple of folded pieces of paper tucked inside the pages of the notebook. I took them out and read them.

The first one was a copy of "The Serenity Prayer":

God, Grant me the Serenity
to accept the things I cannot change,
the courage to change the things I can,
and the wisdom to know the difference.

Whoa. Why would Jess have a prayer in his notebook?

And why this one—it almost seemed like a joke to me, the way it was everywhere, plastered on things wherever you went. Did Jess actually take it seriously?

The other paper was even more bizarre: it was a printout of the "Word of the Day" from some religious website. The topic was "Letting Go and Letting God." It talked about imagining a river, and putting all your troubles into the current—watching them flow away, toward God.

I couldn't imagine Jess buying into this. I almost wanted to wake him up, to demand some sort of explanation.

But of course I didn't.

Not only would I never disturb him, but I could never let him know I was reading his private stuff. He'd never told me *not* to look at it, but it was wrong—I hadn't asked. I couldn't tell him—couldn't take the chance he'd get mad.

I stuck the papers back where I'd found them.

Then I looked at the last poem in the book. It was called "Sam":

Selene Castrovilla

Eternity, evermore
That's how long your love is for
Angel beside me, saving grace
Sunlight shining on your face
The world, my world is what you are
Guiding me, a shining star
A rainbow reigning over me
Brightening the sky, all I see
Passion and goodness, lover and friend
You hold me when my heart descends

The missing piece to my puzzle
The key to unlock my door
I'll love you from the heavens
for eternity,

Evermore.

I put the notebook back and grabbed a tissue from Jess's bedside box.

I held his hand until visiting hours ended. He didn't wake up, didn't even flinch the whole time. I left him a note, a drawing, actually: a heart, with another heart inside of it.

My version of a poem.

Chapter 21

"Ever think about God?" Jess asked me.

Oh yes I do.

I'd been contemplating God often since reading that stuff in Jess's notebook—wondering why he had it in there. But I didn't know how he'd feel about my looking at it, so I didn't tell him.

"Think about him how?" I returned vaguely.

Jess was sitting with his laptop, on the cancer website again. He'd been on it for hours, ever since coming back from the hospital this morning. "Well, in the universal sense, I guess. I mean, I don't think there's a guy in a robe with a long white beard up in the clouds, but it seems like there's something guiding us and the world, doesn't it?"

"I don't know." I bit my lip. If there was something up there, why was it hurting Jess?

It was like he'd read my mind. "Remember in the park, you asked me if I thought God did this to me? Well, that stayed with me. Then I found a section of posts on the site debating God. I've been reading them ever since."

"Religiously?" I asked. I couldn't resist.

He laughed, though I wasn't sure if I'd meant to be funny. "Yeah, you could say that. Anyway, after much consideration, I can honestly say I don't believe that God—or whatever you want to call what's out there—has it in for me."

I didn't say anything; this was a lot for me to handle at the moment—though I wasn't sure why. It was like I was teetering on some abyss. . . .

"Basically, I've decided to stop caring," he said.

"That doesn't sound good."

"But I mean it in a good way, Sam—I'm not trying to control what I can't—which is pretty much everything. A lot of the people on here call it surrendering."

"Surrender?" I thought of that message on the hallway ceiling—not a pleasant thought.

"Like in the twelve steps."

"Aren't those for alcoholics?"

"Yes, but some of the ideas in them work for people with cancer. Especially step three."

"What's that?"

"Make a decision to turn our will and our lives over to the care of God as we understand Him."

I stared at him for a long moment. "I cannot believe you know that by heart. You sound like a robot."

"I'm not a robot, Sam. I just think about this a lot." He sounded hurt.

I was rude. Here he was feeling good, better than he'd been in forever, and I was picking on him for memorizing something that mattered to him. "I'm sorry, Jess. This is just . . . a bit much. You know?"

"I know." He reached over, gave my leg a squeeze. "Don't worry—I'm not some Jesus freak. I've just . . . made my peace with God."

"Great."

"I guess it does sound odd." He smiled, and I was glad. It was a terrific smile—I hadn't seen one like that on him in so long.

He did in fact seem peaceful. Why was I feeling so the opposite? I couldn't imagine cracking a smile; I'd forgotten what it felt like.

"So . . . what religion are you?" I asked him.

"No religion. I'm just spiritual."

"Do you actually pray?" I asked. It seemed strange to even say the word.

He nodded. "Yup."

"How do you . . . start?"

"I say the Serenity Prayer. You know what that is?"

"Yeah. I've seen it on pillows and magnets, stuff like that." And in his notebook, of course, but I couldn't tell him that.

"Then I just launch right in." He laughed. "I say how grateful I am."

"Grateful?" That was too much. "How can you be grateful? Grateful for what?"

He shrugged. "I'm grateful for everything. For you, for the sun and the air, for each moment—I just feel grateful. It's like a load's been lifted off of me."

"Oh, yeah? Are you grateful for cancer?"

Oh, God. What a snide, mean bitch I was.

But he wasn't mad.

"I know it's hard for you to understand, Sam. I wish I could give you this feeling—share it with you." He really did sound like one of those religious zealots and it scared me. Was he going to start quoting scripture next?

We sat in silence for a little while.

He took my hand and I concentrated on that—on that warmth, on that beat going between us. I wanted to understand, but it was impossible; it was like he was speaking in tongues. All I felt was sadness and anger.

Then he said, "I forgave my dad."

"How? You haven't even spoken to him."

"That's the thing—I didn't need to. I just released everything." He squeezed into my hand. "I just turned it all over to my higher power."

"That's wonderful, Jess."

And of course I meant it—I wanted him to be happy and feel good, obviously—but somehow I was also feeling abandoned. It was like Jess was leaving me for God.

"What's going on with your dad?" he asked me.

"Still dead," I said. "Oh, God—that was awful. I'm sorry, Jess." It was the second time I'd apologized in the conversation. He let go of my hand. I couldn't blame him. *What's wrong with me?*

He said, "I was just wondering if you were still seeing him, and if you'd told your mom."

"Yes, and no."

"I wish you'd talk to her."

"I can't imagine how that would help." Plus, I didn't want to burden her with any additional mental issues I had. "Maybe I'll just pray for an answer."

He looked at me for a moment. "I don't expect you to get it, but maybe you could just respect that I've found something that brings me relief, okay?"

That sounded so reasonable. Why was it so hard?

"I'll try," I told him.

I went to my mom. Not to tell her about glimpsing my dad—I really didn't want to lay that on her. It probably was just dreaming anyway—except I was awake when it happened.

It was daydreaming. That's all.

Anyway, I wasn't going to discuss Dad. *But this new thing with Jess* . . . How was I supposed to compete with God?

"Oh, baby," Mom said, after I told her about what Jess had revealed. "You're not competing with anyone. I'm just happy that Jesse feels better."

"Me, too. But—he's talking about all these things— it's like he's a different person."

We were sitting at her kitchen table with a plate of several kinds of cookies between us. What would Mom ever do without her trusty oven? It was incredible that she wasn't fat; but then, she was always offering her baked goods to everyone else. She never really ate any of it herself.

"People discover things, Sam. Their tastes change, and people grow. No one's stagnant. You aren't, either, even if you might feel that way right now."

Funny that Mom would say this, wearing her usual sweats; she was pretty stagnant herself. Was it still grief, or did she devote so much energy to my brother and me, and her books, that she had nothing left to try doing something new, or different? Maybe one day I could talk to her about that—when I wasn't so wrapped up in myself and Jess.

"I get what you're saying, Mom. But this—it's like God's taken him over." I played with the plate of cookies, rotating it.

"It's a unique situation, I'll admit. But if this works for him, you have to find a way to support him in it. Maybe you can learn more about it yourself."

I was shocked. "You want me to find God? You, who raised me with no religion?"

"I'm not completely faithless. I've just never been comfortable with organized religion. And I guess with everything that's gone on in our lives, I never addressed it with you. I'm sorry if I shortchanged you on this."

I stopped spinning the plate and took a cookie, choosing an oatmeal raisin cookie with burnt edges and not too many raisins—though you never could tell for sure.

"Are you saying you buy into this God stuff in some way?"

"I'm not ruling anything out, baby. And if it makes him happy, that's a good thing."

I held the cookie, feeling its craggy surface. But I didn't raise it to my lips; I didn't really feel like eating it. It was more like a prop—something to hold on to.

"I'm afraid . . . I'm scared he's going to change so much that I'll lose him. . . ."

She reached across the table, put her palm over my hand without disturbing my grip on the cookie, and squeezed.

"You know what Roosevelt said: 'The only thing we have to fear is fear itself.' Think about that, Sam."

Walking through Oz and back to Jess, I did think about that. And when I got inside his room again, I apologized. I promised him, and myself, that I would work on respecting his new beliefs—and accepting that he was still the same in his heart.

I had to learn to believe there was room in his heart for both me *and* God.

It took me a week of working on it, but finally I felt reassured that I wasn't losing Jess to God. But I *was* losing him to his friends.

It was two a.m. and Jess wasn't home yet; he'd gone out at around seven to see a movie with Pete and the guys, and I wasn't invited. Well, it's not like they'd said I wasn't, but they hadn't asked me to go, either. I would've ignored that detail a year ago, but now I realized that guys needed guy-time; I didn't especially like it, but I recognized it.

Since Jess had been sprung from the hospital, he'd gone out with his friends four times. But who was counting? It was like he was either busy with his cancer support people, praying, or going out—and none of it included me.

Meanwhile, I sat entombed in Gwen's bathroom; it had the warmth of a mausoleum. A few minutes earlier, I'd woken up for about the seventeenth time to find Jess's bed still empty. I'd stumbled into the bathroom, slammed up the shiny black toilet seat cover, sat, and peed. That meant facing the hideous painting hanging across from the toilet: a man and a woman, both dressed in black, each with most of their faces missing. She only had eyes—really mournful blue eyes. He had only a huge grin, like the Joker. They were in a dark forest with bare trees; a bowl of fruit rested in the dirt at their feet, with a big carving knife jabbed into an apple. What a thing to hang in a bathroom. Or anywhere. That painting never failed to get to me, but it especially did at times like this—lonely, two a.m. times.

God, I sucked—getting jealous like this, wanting Jess here, all to myself. I guess I could've called my girlfriends, but I didn't. I'd never been as close with them as I was with Jess, and it seemed like such an effort to pick up the phone. And it wasn't like they were begging to hang out with me or anything when I'd see them at school. Who knew if they even wanted to be friends anymore? Who knew if I did?

No, I didn't want to chat with my supposed friends, didn't want to go and do "the girl thing," whatever that meant. Socializing was something I'd never quite fathomed. I only wanted to be with Jess. But Jess had other plans.

Miserable wench! I cursed myself as I hunched on that toilet seat staring into the forest of doom. But I missed him. Was this what it was going to be like now? Was he slipping away from me? Had he ever really been mine, or was I just convenient?

Don't, I begged my mind. *Don't go there*. It wasn't true, couldn't be true. Two a.m. rantings were never logical, never right.

Were they?

But Jess was gone, and my rantings were all I had to keep me company. Them and a wretched painting from hell. The grey granite floor was cold and biting against my bare feet, sending a chill through my body. I shivered, forced myself up from the toilet, and flushed. Twisting the gleaming brass faucet, I blasted the hot water into the black and gold marble sink and splashed my face. *If I wash myself enough, maybe I can get all the bad thoughts out and get back to sleep.*

Yeah, right.

By the time I stepped back into the bedroom, my most selfish thoughts were whooping through my mind again, like Indians doing a rain dance. *When Jess goes for the chemo, he'll come back to me. He'll need me to take care of him.*

How horrible was that—to think such a thing, to look forward to it?

I clutched at Jess's balled pillow, a poor substitute for him, but at least it had his scent. I needed to smell him to sleep. Mashing that fluff against my nose and inhaling was a relief, the way a fish must feel, released from a hook and given a second chance at breathing. I was completely dependent on Jesse and it appalled me. I wasn't sure if I'd even stop sleeping with Jess if I found out that he was using me—or that I *could* stop. *Pathetic*.

But I loved him. He said he loved me, he wrote that

damn poem about me. But where was he, now that he was feeling better?

Where was he?

Why wasn't I good enough to be with when he was well?

I squeezed into the pillow tighter, tighter, until I'd squished my fingers right into the center and there was no more to squish. I pressed it against my face; it was like an oxygen mask on a plane. Dr. Chadwick had talked about fastening the mask around your own face first, before trying to help someone else. But there was no one else to take care of now, and the plane was going down. Who would rescue me?

Sleep, I willed myself. *Sleep. Things will look different in the morning.*

And even if they didn't, I had to face the facts. I had no one to blame for all this but myself. I was the one who'd slipped into Jess's bed to begin with, not the other way around.

Yeah, that was it exactly. *It hadn't been the other way around.* The words whipped through my head. No matter what he said, it probably never would've been.

I rumpled into the pillow, but it was no good now. Now, it felt like a shroud of cotton and feathers.

All I wanted to do was fade out, but I couldn't.

I put the pillow down and stared ahead in the dark. Light would help, I thought, so I flicked the lamp on. Then I noticed Kitty's button eyes staring at me accusingly from the far corner of the bed. "Pull yourself together," she'd tell me if she weren't an inanimate object. But what did Kitty know anyway? She'd been coming apart at the seams for years. I turned away and sunk back into the mush of Jess's pillow.

To sleep, to wipe out all the hurt. To forget, at least for a while, at least until the sun came back. But it was impossible—to sleep, or forget.

I felt like I was going mad, and then I got further evidence of it.

There was a new scent in the room now—an impossible scent. It was my dad's cologne—one I'd gotten him for his birthday. The last birthday he'd had, and the last gift from me.

Oh, God. How could it be? Was I really crazy?

Somehow smelling him was worse than all those times seeing him. It gave more dimension to his presence. The scent made him more real.

I pushed the pillow aside, kicked off the covers, and fled.

I stumbled through the dark to the other side of the apartment, to Maria's room. I didn't dare turn on the lights and risk disturbing Gwen. In my panic I ran into several pieces of furniture, but I managed to keep it quiet.

I had to talk to Maria.

My freaked-out meter was higher than any concern about the wrath of Gwen if I woke her, and I rapped on the door. Logically I knew I could make a little noise here—it was a safe distance from Gwen's room—but still I cringed at the sounds I made.

"Sammy, wat is it?" Maria said, swinging her door open wide to let me in. She was in a bright turquoise flannel nightgown, with several pairs of multicolored beads strung around her neck. I'd be afraid of choking in my sleep with those things on, but she thought of them as protection against evil spirits. I knew because she'd told me so a long time ago; back then it seemed crazy to do the things she did. Now, I would've been willing to bargain with the devil. That's the kind of thing that happened in the dead of night, I supposed, when people were still awake. The night was meant for sleeping.

Maria's bare feet poked from under the hem. She'd come to the door without stopping to put on her slippers. I realized how rude I was being, jarring her from bed like that.

"I'm sorry, Maria. This was the only place I could go—"

"Shhh, of course you come here. You can always come here, Sammy," she said, dismissing my apology with a wave of her hand. She held the door open for me, and I went inside. It'd been a long time since I'd been there—years.

"Jess isn't home yet," I explained. We sat on the edge of her white bedspread, and I poured out my troubles. I stopped short of telling her about my dad. It probably was all in my head anyway. I was stressed to the max, hallucinating—and now smelling my dad, too.

God, I needed to get a grip.

Maria's small room was like a shrine. There were lit candles everywhere, which might've been romantic if not for the crosses and the giant picture of Jesus on one wall, which was surrounded with candles. The scent of Go Away, Evil! spray hung in the air.

"You worried 'bout Jesse?"

"No, I—" No, just about losing him . . . I didn't want to say it out loud, but then I looked into Jesus' sad eyes and it all came pouring out.

"Oh, Sammy. He loves you."

That startled me—until I realized she meant Jess, of course.

"I know he does, but—" *Well, what does love mean anyway? Nothing substantial—nothing you can hold on to.*

"What you need is a coconut shell reading," Maria counseled. She patted my hand.

Why not?

"We will ask Ochum for an answer," Maria said. "She's the Goddess of Love."

"Okay," I said. Might as well ask the Goddess of Love. It fit the situation.

"Her colors are yellow, gold, and orange," Maria said. "I have beads in her colors. You must wear them."

"Whatever you say." I allowed her to drape three strands of plastic beads over my head—one necklace in each of the goddess's colors. They went well with my Happy Bunny pajamas. The thing about this was, I was actually taking it seriously, hoping for some kind of answers. But what even was the question?

Maybe Maria asked the goddess a question, but I

couldn't know what it was because she was chanting in some other language and sprinkling water on the floor. Then she tossed four pieces of coconut shell onto the green carpet. They landed noiselessly, one with the curve facing up, the other three curves facing down.

"*Itagua!*" Maria pronounced—whatever that meant. "It means 'probably yes,' but we have to ask again," she explained.

I still didn't know what the question was, but I was willing to go along with her, rather than sit back in Jess's bedroom alone.

She did it again; again, we got the same results.

"Unbelievable!" she said.

I don't know that I would've called it unbelievable. It was like rolling snake eyes twice. It happens.

"Maybe we're not meant to know the answer just yet," I suggested.

Maria stared at me hard, in consideration. "You may be right, Sammy," she said. "But I tink we try da seashells now."

She opened a little jar and sprinkled a bunch of little shells into her palm. Again, she recited something with great vehemence and intention. Whatever she was saying, she meant it.

She tossed the shells onto the carpet. They made no noise at all.

We both looked at them. I didn't know what they stood for, so I just counted them.

There were fifteen. Some up, some down.

"The answer is ordun number eight," Maria said.

"What does that mean?"

"The seashells don't give answers, they give advice. Yours are telling you 'The head carries the body.' "

"Ah." I said. "Well, thanks." That was about as useful as the last fortune I'd gotten from a cookie: "Blood flows through the veins." Maybe all this meant that I needed to pay closer attention in biology.

"I tink you need an herbal love bath," Maria said. "I go run it for you."

I couldn't imagine taking a bath at that moment; I was feeling kind of sleepy, maybe from the flickering of the candles.

"Maybe tomorrow," I told her. "I think I'm gonna go now. But I feel better—thanks."

"If tings get worse, we can write your names on paper, prick your finger, circle your names in your blood, and bury the paper precisely at nine o'clock on Friday night," she said as I rose.

I gave her a hug. "I'll keep that in mind, Maria."

I realized I never did find out what she'd asked the goddess of the coconut shells, or whoever it was. But then, we hadn't gotten a solid answer, anyway. It was like the Magic Eight Ball when it said "Ask again later." There was a lot of that in life, especially lately.

I stepped away from Maria's room like an exhausted Mardi Gras celebrator with my heavy eyes and my strands of beads.

What would Gwen think if she knew what was going on in Maria's bedroom? It wouldn't be anything good.

❄

I didn't say anything to Jess the next day—about missing him, about my dad, or about the strange rituals in Maria's room. I was just glad to see him, and relieved that the night was gone. But I didn't see much of him. He slept most of the day, rising only when Maria prodded and poked him, and then only long enough to sit up, eat a piece of toast, and take his meds.

He fell back onto his pillow, spoke to me for a little while about the movie, some kind of cop versus psycho thriller. His voice faded little by little, and he was back to nighty-night land. Of course he was tired—he wasn't used to going out, or doing anything but lie around—and then there was the cancer, eating at his strength as well. It wouldn't have been so bad if I could've snuggled up to him, but of course that was impossible with Gwen home.

I spent the day studying math, at least as much as I could. It was so hard to concentrate, to think of anything but Jess. He'd promised to keep me company, to help me pass everything, and there he was, unconscious from a night of who knew what?

Think trig, I commanded myself. I stared at hordes of numbers, squinting to focus as they wriggled and swam before me and my head grew heavier, heavier, heavier. . . .

"Sam?"

"Huh?" I jolted up from the bed, knocking the trig book to the floor and drooling out of the left side of my mouth. Obviously I hadn't gotten very far studying.

"Sorry," Jess said. "Didn't mean to scare you."

"'S'okay." I wiped my mouth and picked the book up, then climbed back onto the bed.

"Come over here, will you?" He patted next to him. Sure, now he wanted me, when he felt nice and refreshed and I was worn out from worry—and exhausted from coconut rituals.

I went.

He draped his arm around me, kissed me. "How's it going?"

I thought about telling him how it was going—how lonely I was, and how, as trite as it sounded, my heart literally ached for him when he wasn't there. I thought about telling him about two a.m. in the bathroom, and about how unbearably hard it was to be alone in the dark. I thought about telling him all the thoughts I'd had in that terrible night so he'd prove them wrong, or at least have the chance to.

But instead, I said, "Fine."

Who knew where to begin, where to end, whether it was right to feel the way I did? It was all so overwhelming, and so the only thing to do was nothing.

"Cool," he said.

He told me again about the movie, more coherently this time. Then he told me they went to an all-night coffee bar afterward, which had a pool table, too. It all seemed harmless enough, this boys' night out. I was feeling better, until he slipped in his revelation: Cindy had been there.

"Cindy?" I repeated. "You invited Cindy?" *And not me?* The last part of the question made it out of my brain, but not out of my mouth.

"I didn't invite her, Sam. She showed up at Where Ya Bean—that was the name of the coffee bar—and just started playing with us."

"How could she just start playing? Someone had to share his cue."

"Sam." He cut me off, looked at me intently. "I told you because I want to be completely honest. I didn't invite her; I barely spoke with her. Okay?"

It damn well wasn't okay, but what could I say? I'd certainly hung out enough with Jess when she was dating him. Turnabout totally sucked.

"Sam . . . say something." He looked upset, like he wanted forgiveness. Did he need to be forgiven for something?

"Okay." I patted his leg, rested my hand there. "Okay."

He smiled then, and stroked my cheek. "Thanks for not making it a big deal."

My hand tensed up on his leg, squeezing tight. I covered quickly by continuing the action—massaging his muscle, like that was what I'd meant to do.

If he only knew what's going on inside.

Chapter 22

Things stayed like that for the next week: me tense and lonely, and hating myself for being tense and lonely; and him barely there, and sleeping most of the time when he was. I dealt with it silently, partly because I didn't want to fight with him, but partly because I wasn't sure I had the right to my feelings.

And I said nothing mostly because he was starting chemo again, and then everything would change.

But the thing with Cindy irked me the most. I kind of wished I could talk to Pete about her again; he was the first person to cut through my jealousy with any efficiency. It was like using a sharpened pair of scissors after years of struggling with those dull, rounded-edge blades on the kiddie ones. But I was kind of pissed at Pete, too, for not including me in his plans with Jess. Stupid and irrational, yeah; I knew my thinking was both. The guy owed me nothing. He was Jess's friend, not mine. I just thought we'd bonded a bit, I guess.

Jess didn't mention Cindy again and I didn't bring her

up. I assumed she hadn't showed up again, and that he'd have told me if she had, but I didn't want to sound jealous by asking.

It was the night before chemo. Jess was staying home—storing up his energy on the off chance that a well-rested body would respond better to the chemo, or at least feel the side effects less.

He was sinking already, mentally—even spiritually. It was like he was afraid that if he allowed himself to hope he'd respond better to the treatment this time, then it'd be that much further for him to fall if it was just as bad as before, or worse.

Poor Jess.

I'd decided to surprise him with a picnic dinner like the one we'd had on prom night, only this time we'd dine in his room so he didn't have to go anywhere.

During the day I'd been at the library, doing research for a paper on Charles Darwin that I had to hand in at the end of the summer. I'd just learned that Darwin's wife had been extremely religious and had agonized about her husband's soul. I guess it's in women's nature, to worry about their men.

I'd told Jess I'd be back late, but that was before I came up with my brilliant idea. I closed the books early, picked up the food at the deli two blocks from our building, and packed it up at home.

With the stuffed basket on one arm and the sparkling cider clutched in the other hand, I opened the door to Jess's apartment and then, after walking the corridor from hell, swung the door to his room. I saw Jess's trophies—the gold, silver, and bronze statues standing tall across the room where they always waited when I walked in.

Then my gaze fell lower. There was someone on the bed with Jess, back toward me, blocking Jess from view. Someone with long hair. Long auburn hair with highlights.

She turned, smirked—a huge smirk.

I saw Jess's face now, his horrified face.

And lipstick.

Lipstick!

Pink lipstick on his lips. His lips moved; he said something, but I couldn't hear. I saw pink and that was all I could manage.

My feet moved me in, dragged me halfway across the floor. I tried to digest, to see another way the pink could've gotten smeared all over his lips. But there was no other way.

He spoke. I didn't hear him.

She smirked, smirked, smirked.

Cindy smirked.

"Bastard," I said. The bottle was heavy, wet, and cold in my hand. I heaved it. It connected with the picture on the bedside table, the one from senior movie night, the one I'd rescued, the one with the cracks that Jess had never wanted to look at before. Plastic crunched, metal clanked, and it crashed to the floor, demolished.

Good, I thought. *Good*.

But the thrill of destruction was gone in a moment, re-placed with the ache of despair. "Bastard," I repeated, drop-ping to my knees. The basket slipped from my arm; I left it there on the floor, tried to get up but couldn't focus, couldn't process the thoughts I needed to rise. I looked up and saw her again, with her grin.

I clamped my eyes tight and crawled blindly, banging into things, until finally, mercifully, I felt the hard bump of the threshold under my knees. I opened my eyes, faced the hallway with its leering paintings—a long path to nowhere. *Purgatory*, I thought, and I didn't even believe in that stuff. But if I did, I knew Purgatory would look like Gwen's heartless hall.

Maria stepped out in her red terry robe and pink feath-ered slippers—a valentine blocking my way.

"Sammy? What happen? Why you on da floor?" She reached down and helped me up.

I heard Jess calling me now. Damned if I was turning back, setting foot in that room I'd just slithered from. Here I'd thought it was Eden; did that make me the serpent?

"I'm leaving." My chest felt heavy and it was hard to breathe. Somewhere behind me, nearer than before, Jess called my name. He was coming after me, as fast as he could.

I detached my hand from Maria's. "I'm going."

Maria looked beyond me into Jess's room. She must've spotted Cindy, because she muttered something fast and Spanish, then said, "Stay, Sammy. Talk to him."

"Sam—" Jess was close now, like he was practically on top of me.

"I'm leaving," I told Maria.

And I left.

I was beyond tears when I stepped onto the sidewalk. An icy heaviness had built up inside me, but otherwise I felt nothing. I knew where I was going—to the only haven I had. Back to our sanctuary—now a crime scene, roped off with yellow tape in my mind.

All those lies he'd told me. Had he meant anything he'd said?

I trudged into the park, plodded down the dimly lit path, then clumped across grass, breathing in its too-sweet, too-fresh smell until I reached the spot, our former stretch of happiness bordered by the three lofty trees. Once our place in the sun, and later our place in the stars.

The sun had set. The twinkling lights were gone. It was all I had left, that dark patch of grass, that lonely bit of earth. No one could take that from me.

I slumped at the foot of a tree, gnarled bark scratching my back. I curled into a ball on the chilly soil and slept.

"Sam, Sam!"

Someone was touching me, warm fingers on my frigid skin.

"Sam, are you okay?"

That voice . . .

Something warm was covering me now—a blanket? It was soothing . . . I came out of my muddled, restless dreams and opened my eyes, even more confused. My hair was tangled around my face like blinders, but through it I could see that it wasn't a blanket wrapped around me. It was Jesse.

"Oh, thank God," he said. "You were so cold!"

"Why are you here?"

"Why am I here? Because you're here."

He didn't have the lipstick on him anymore—he must've washed it off. But my mind drew the pink right back on those lips.

"Shouldn't you be with Cindy?"

He smoothed my hair out of my face, then kissed me. I wanted to pull away, but I didn't. "I'm sorry, Sam. I'm sorry you walked in just at that moment."

"Yeah, me too." I tried looking away, but there was no escaping his eyes when they wanted my attention.

Jerk.

Why did I have to love him?

"*She* kissed me, *Sam*."

"I got that." A tear trickled out. *So much for being past tears.* Stupid jerk.

He pressed his lips against my cheek, sucked in my tear. I wanted to pull back, but I didn't. Big stupid jerk.

"Sam, I didn't kiss her back."

"What?"

"I didn't kiss her back. I would've told her to leave if you hadn't walked in."

"What?"

184

"Sam, I love *you*."

The ice inside me melted and I cried again.

"Don't cry anymore, Sam. I'm always making you cry." His lips roved my skin now.

How can I believe him? Trust him?

How can I ever know he really loves me?

"Marry me, Sam."

The absurdity of the words smacked into my brain. *Marry him?* We were teenagers. It was ridiculous. But the romanticism in the words . . . it was there, too. Undeniably.

He wanted to marry me.

I softened, loosened, and released the sorrow and pain I'd carried to the park.

He wanted to marry me.

He kissed me still, leaned against my tired, chilled body—true protection against the dark elements. I breathed in his scent deeply; it was like smelling the first spring blossoms. And I felt what, a short while ago, I was sure I'd never feel again.

I felt hope.

Chapter 23

"So?" Maria asked. "Is everybody 'appy now?"

Jess and I were back in his room, in his bed. Maria had come in with a box of chocolates and waved it at us. She *really* looked like a valentine now. I'd taken what I hoped was a caramel. Jess had passed on it.

"Are you happy, Sam?" Jess asked, squeezing into me.

I nodded. I was feeling grounded and loved. I *was* happy.

My stomach growled loudly, apparently awakened by the sugar and fluff I'd ingested—it turned out to be marshmallow.

"Jesus, Sammy!" Maria exclaimed. "Don' you eat nuttin' today?"

I remembered the picnic we were supposed to have. The picture and cider were gone—Maria must've cleaned up—but the basket was still sitting on the floor next to the wheelchair, unopened.

"I meant to," I said, salivating at the basket. I told them about my plans.

"Don' you worry 'bout nuttin'," Maria said with a wink. "You two stay here, I make you plates of chicken." She grabbed the basket and headed to the kitchen.

And for the first time in what felt like forever, I wasn't worried about anything. I felt light.

Jess stroked my cheek. "You didn't answer me," he said. His voice had a slight tremor. "Does that mean no?"

I turned to face Jess and gazed into those warm hazel eyes. They were like hot chocolate by a fire on a cold winter's day; they were home. He was home to me, he was my Kansas. I'd known it as far back as I could remember knowing things. I probably knew it the first time those elevator doors opened and I faced him in his stroller.

And now he wanted to marry me—just push aside all the obvious problems that went with the question and marry me. There was time to worry about how's and if's, to pile all that on top of the other things we were dealing with.

For tonight I was willing to suspend disbelief.

"Yes, Jess. I'll marry you."

The next day I held Jesse's hand while the lab technician injected the chemo drugs into his chest. I squeezed his hand and felt his pulse beating wildly in his fingers. The tech plunged the syringe into the tube—the tube that Jess had sworn didn't hurt him, but I could tell it did.

It did, even if he didn't feel it. It was a violation, a constant violation.

Our eyes locked as the drugs entered his bloodstream on their seek-and-destroy mission, annihilating everything, the bad and the good. They were soldiers obeying orders without question.

I was ripped apart watching his eyes fill with surrender, submitting to the drugs, succumbing to their purpose—to their fierce devastation as they launched their attack, bombarding his cells and blitzing his body.

The tech finished up and left the room. I held Jess, pressed his head against my chest while the drugs advanced through his veins.

I held Jess while he cried.

Chapter 24

Jess had been right not to get his hopes up. He got sick from the chemo immediately, and by the time a week went by, he was in worse shape than he'd ever been. It was torture to see him suffer each morning, to watch him wake and remember all over again.

It was Monday, the start of Jess's third week of chemo. "Morning," I said when he woke up. He'd been sleeping later; whether from exhaustion or indifference, I couldn't say. I mustered a smile.

"Morning." He attempted to smile but couldn't pull it off. He just had nothing to smile about. True, he wasn't heaving anymore, but he was so weak. His fear had been realized; some days, he couldn't walk.

A chill slid through me and I shivered. Despite the heat of the summer, a/c and I were not compatible.

"Can you—do you need help, Jess?" I knew he had to go to the bathroom, one way or another.

He hoisted himself up slowly, winced, then sank back down. I went over to him, gave him a kiss.

"What do you want to do, hon?" I asked. "You want to try to walk with me?"

It was hard to say which Jess hated more of the other two choices—the wheelchair or the bedpan. He twisted his sheet in his hand, nodded.

I lowered the bar on the side of the bed—I'd finally mastered it. Then I leaned against him and he wrapped his arms around me. I boosted him up, trying not to react to his groaning and trembling—he hated that—and pulled him as gently as I could from the bed.

It was hard supporting his weight; I could have gotten help from Maria, and possibly even Gwen, but I knew Jess would rather keep his struggle between us.

We limped across the room, through the doorway, and into the bathroom. Then I waited outside the door for him. Afterward, we repeated the effort in reverse. The hardest part was getting him back into bed without hurting him too much.

Actually, that wasn't true. The hardest part was holding back my tears, seeing Jess like that—knowing how absolutely miserable and degraded he felt. Never mind the horrific pain he was in.

I smoothed the covers over him and flipped his flopped-over kitty back and upright against the wall.

"You feel like breakfast, Jess?"

He shrugged, then stared at the red stripes on the wallpaper.

"How 'bout a breakfast bar?"

"I guess." His voice was low and he still wouldn't look at me.

"Sweetheart—" Tangy anguish twisted inside me as I fought to find words for him. Everything sounded so damn false. It was like Dr. Chadwick said—trite clichés did nothing. So I said the one thing that rang true: "I love you."

"I love you, too," he quietly told the wall.

When I came back, Jess was still staring at stripes. "Jess?"

He looked at me—at least that was something.

I gave him the breakfast bar, then put a glass of milk and his meds on his nightstand. "Thanks," he said softly.

"Are you gonna study today?"

He shrugged. "I don't think so. You go ahead, though."

"That's what you said for the last three days. How are you going to get everything done?"

He shrugged again. "Who cares, anyway?"

"Jess . . . all right, I'm not going to argue with you. But will you at least come sit with me in the park?"

"No."

"Why?"

"Sam." His eyes moved to the wheelchair, and if he could've, I knew he'd have shot out lasers to disintegrate it. "I'm not going anywhere in that."

"I'll walk you out."

"Oh, come on. You're not that strong. I'm practically killing you with my bathroom trips."

"No, you're not." I took his hand. "Please?"

I hated that look in his eyes, that hollow look. Just past sad, just short of defeat. But at least he held my stare.

I climbed into bed next to him, pressed close and felt his heart pounding. I risked a real kiss, in broad daylight. Gwen would have gotten quite the eyeful.

"Okay," he said, many heartbeats later. "And—might as well bring a book for me, too."

Gwen blocked the hallway like a stiff sentry. She thought it was absurd for us to walk to the park and told us so in her usual diplomatic way. She said we should take the wheelchair, and that's why it was there. And just the mention of that stupid chair struck Jess dumb.

I said we'd manage just fine and guided him past her. Then Maria popped her head from the kitchen and offered to help, but I said no thanks.

Once out the door, we kept having to stop and take breathers, leaning against walls, furnishings in the building, and the brick facade outside before making the sluggish journey across the street.

Finally, we were there. And it was worth it—what a spectacular day to be in the park. The shade cooled things off, the air was sweet with the scents of flowers and grilled sausages, and the birds were doing their chirpy thing. *Zippity-do-dah*.

We didn't go to our spot—it was too far; but I settled

for a big, thick tree to sit under, near the entrance. I propped Jess against it and sat facing him, unpacking our books.

"Comfortable?" I asked, handing him the play he had to read for English: Shakespeare's "Henry the Fourth, Part II." He'd just finished part one when he got sick in January.

"Uh . . . yeah," he said. I understood—he was as comfortable as he was going to get.

I took out my math book and tried to concentrate.

"Hey," Jess said softly. "Sam."

I looked up. "Yeah?"

"I still wanna do it, you know."

"Do what?"

"Get married."

I put the book down in the grass, moved close to him, and held him. He looked so sad, so lost, like a kid determined to do something, but with no idea how.

We hadn't talked about getting married since the night before he started the chemo. He'd gotten sick so fast. I'd wondered if he'd forgotten his proposal, or maybe changed his mind. Either way, there didn't seem a reason to bring it up. And really, it seemed so hopeless, the idea of us getting married. How could we? It'd been enough that he'd asked, that he'd wanted to marry me. It'd been enough to put me at ease, to know that he truly cared that much.

"I'm sorry I haven't talked more about it. It's just . . . I've been so sick."

"It's okay, Jess," I said, taking his hand in mine, interlocking our fingers.

"But we need to plan. . . . "

Could he really mean to go through with it—to actually get married?

"Sweetheart, we can't get married without permission."

"So, then we'll get permission."

The thought occurred to me that the chemo had affected his brain.

"Jess, your mom isn't going to let us get married."

"Why not?"

Is he serious? "Have you met Gwen?" I asked.

"She's been cool, she's been better lately."

"Not *that* cool."

"We'll see," he said, squeezing my hand.

It was nice, his planning our wedding. I just hoped his intentions didn't come crashing down like everything else had.

"We'll see," he repeated as his pulse beat into my palm.

The opportunity to see just how cool Gwen was came sooner than expected when we woke up the next morning and found her glaring at us.

How could I have fallen asleep with Jess? Stupid, stupid.

"Isn't this a lovely sight," she said.

"It is, actually," Jess told her.

"Is what?" she asked.

"It is a lovely sight," Jess said. This was it—he was

coming clean about us. His tone wasn't daring or confronting, it wasn't snotty or sarcastic. It was strong and clear, and it said "enough."

Gwen wasn't sure what to make of this so she waited for more, saying nothing.

"Mom, the last time you found Sam and me in bed, when I said we weren't lovers, it was true. We weren't."

Gwen raised her eyebrows at what she had to know was coming next, but she kept quiet.

"But things happen, and then people realize what they maybe should've figured out sooner but didn't. And then things change."

Gwen blinked, elevated her brows even farther, but still said nothing.

"Mom, Sam's my girlfriend now." As if to provide a visual to further explain, Jess took my shaking hand in his. I was freaked, sure that this was the end of my staying over.

Gwen cleared her throat. Then she swallowed saliva. I watched her gulp and I waited: would the woman ever speak?

Finally, she did. "I see."

There was a great silence as we all took in the implications.

Then she said, "It would've been nice if you could have . . . been honest . . . told me. . . ." Her voice trailed off.

"You weren't very open to honesty, Mom," Jess said.

"Right," she said, then cleared her throat again. "Well, then . . . " She turned away, like she was leaving.

"Mom," Jess said. She turned back, looked at him.

"Things are different with us now, too. I'm sorry I wasn't honest with you."

She nodded. Then she said, "I bought you some Essiac—it's an herb that's supposed to help fight cancer. You make tea with it. That's why I came in here, to see if you wanted some Essiac tea—"

"I'd love some Essiac tea, Mom."

Chapter 25

It was the night before Jess was going back in the hospital for his radiation and stem cell transplant. He was going to be in there for at least three weeks.

He wasn't thrilled, needless to say, but he was glad his chemo was ending.

We were having dinner in the dining room as a send-off. Mom and Teddy were invited, too, and Jess had decided that this would be the perfect time to announce our engagement. I had my doubts, but he'd been further encouraged by Gwen accepting us and not giving me the heave-ho. It *was* nice she'd accepted me as Jess's girlfriend, but . . . girlfriend was a far cry from wife.

We all sat around the long rectangular black lacquered table: Mom, Gwen, Maria, Teddy, Jess, and me. Maria had roasted a turkey and made all kinds of dishes to go with it: stuffing, wild rice with mushrooms, garlic mashed potatoes, sauteed string beans, grilled peppers, corn, salad, and three kinds of pie for dessert.

It was like Thanksgiving in August, except the room

was more Halloweenish: black wallpaper with red flecks, a black lacquered china cabinet to match the table and chairs, a misshapen chandelier with sharpened fragments of glass dangling from it, and more creepy modern art on the walls—The Addams Family goes art deco.

Teddy looked *gawgeous* in Mom's pearls and a fuchsia silk scarf wrapped around his head like a designer babushka. On his feet were my prom shoes, which he'd reminded me the day before that I'd promised he could borrow sometime, and then informed me that yesterday *was* sometime.

I'd dug through my closet, found them buried under an avalanche of novels I'd knocked over searching for something else. They were covered in grass stains and soil, and battered by books—not a pretty sight. I'd handed them over to Ted with trepidation. He inspected them with a frown, then made a disapproving clucking sound.

"Dirty, and crushed," he'd said, glaring at me, but slipped them on anyway and clomp-clomped out of my room.

Tonight Teddy kept us entertained, relieving us from the task of conversation by displaying his vast knowledge of the alphabet, numbers, continents, and French. His pre-K teachers had taught him French words and songs, so we were serenaded as well.

When Maria put out the apple, cherry, and lemon meringue pies, Jess told everyone our news.

"Sam and I want to get married."

He didn't get the response he'd hoped for.

Everyone kind of stared. After a few moments of silence, except for Teddy tapping his fork on the table and humming "Frere Jacques," Maria said, "Good fo' you!" She jumped up, came around the table, and gave each of us a big smooch on our cheeks.

Mom said, "I have to think about this a little. You guys don't understand what it means. . . ."

I'd expected that kind of reaction from Gwen, but not from Mom. "What more do we need to understand, except that we love each other, Mom? It's not like we're going to set up house somewhere."

"Absolutely not!" Gwen jumped from her chair, shoving it back with such force that it teetered and almost fell. She banged her fist on the table, rattling the plates and pies. "Enough of this lunacy! There absolutely will be *no marriage*!"

Teddy got spooked by this. He leapt from his chair and ran from the room, and then Mom threw her napkin down and went after him.

Gwen stood there glowering at Jess and me.

"Mom," Jess said, his voice low and shaking, "Can't—can't you be on our side?"

"No, Jesse. I can't." Then she focused on me. "Isn't it enough, what you have of my son? Do you mean to cut our legal ties as well, to take him away from me completely?"

"Gwen, I—it's not like that—" I sputtered, but before I could get any more words out, she turned her back on us and left the room, leaving Maria, Jess, and me with a whole lot of untouched pie.

❋

Mom coaxed Teddy back into the dining room, which was a lot easier when he saw that Gwen had left. Then Mom cut him a piece of apple pie. No one else felt like eating anymore, and for me, that was saying a lot.

"Mom, did you think about it yet?" I wanted at least one of our parents to approve, and the whole thing was downright depressing at that point.

"Oh, what's the use, Sam?" Jess muttered quietly. He'd been crushed by Gwen's words. "We can't get married without my mom's permission. Just take me to my room, okay?"

I was too down myself to even try to cheer him up. I stood up, then bent to lift him.

"You're right Sam," Mom said. "I *did* think about it, and you're right. I don't know why I hesitated. You two deserve to declare your love publicly, and officially." She nodded her head with approval. "*I* want you to be married."

"Thanks, Mom," I said.

Jesse was still grey. "Yeah, thanks, Ellen. But there's one problem—we need both our parents' consent."

Mom bowed her head. "Sorry I can't help you further, Jesse. But maybe—maybe Gwen'll come around, too."

I hoped so, for Jess's sake even more than for mine.

It meant so much to him, to be my husband. It was like he felt if he could just have that, then he'd have some kind of control again, some kind of power over his own life. I knew he thought it would make up for all the injustices he'd suffered, being sick.

I didn't see it that way, really, but I wanted desperately for him to feel some relief. And I wanted him to have some kind of peace, like the peace he'd given me with his proposal.

And it seemed as though everything hinged around control: Gwen thought I wanted what was left of hers, Jess was struggling to get a smidgen of his back, and once more I felt completely out of control.

Jess and I lay in bed, holding each other. He shifted around, like he just couldn't get comfortable, and his pulse was racing.

"Jess, don't be nervous about tomorrow."

"I'm not—well, okay, I am . . . but it's not that."

"Is it Gwen?"

He shook his head no. "Sam, I made a decision that you need to know, since it affects you, too." He looked so serious.

"What is it?"

He took my hand. "If this clinical trial doesn't pan out, I'm stopping my treatment."

I yanked my hand away and clutched at the covers. "No, Jess!"

"Yes."

I started to say something, but his face told me there was nothing more to say.

"I'm through being a lab rat. I'll do the complementary

medicine, stuff like that, but I'm done with the hospital torture chamber."

I held back my tears. I wanted to be supportive, even though I was feeling a queasy, fracturing kind of pain in my chest, and I knew that my heart was breaking.

"Okay," I whispered, barely able to get the word out.

"You understand, don't you? I want to enjoy my time left with you."

This was it—what I'd really been afraid of.

This was the result of talking to God.

Mom said it wouldn't hurt me—she was *so* wrong.

Jess, spouting on endlessly about gratitude; he had his peace. But what about mine?

I patted his leg, felt the fragments settle inside of me. I simply said, "Okay."

Chapter 26

Two days later, they radiated Jess's entire body.

I went in to see him as soon as he was done. He was sleeping; I should have known he would be. When he'd had radiation on his spine, on the tumor, it'd wiped him out. I could only imagine what having rays sweep through every cell in his body did to him.

I stood just inside the door, staring at his red skin. His words from the other night came hurling back at me, hitting me with a jolt, waking me up.

Jess's decision had made me feel abandoned, and I felt like he'd failed me somehow. But now I wondered: *Have I actually failed him?*

I'd pushed him into that bed, prodded him into fighting for that 4 percent chance, and taken away some of the time he could have enjoyed in the sun. He'd missed out on the sunshine, and yet he looked burned. Now *that* was irony.

Why had I insisted, bullied him into this? For him, or for me? I'd wanted him to fight, and to try everything, but wasn't that selfish when I wasn't the one whose life was at stake?

Why was it so hard to know right from wrong, to see which choices were good ones, or the right ones? For 4 percent, for a supposed cure that so far had cured no one with his kind of cancer. Was it my choice to make?

I stepped closer and he opened his eyes. They were dim, almost extinguished. He gave me a weak smile.

"Hey, sweetheart," I said, giving him a kiss. "I guess I don't have to ask how your day was."

He laughed, but it turned into a cough.

I sat in the chair next to him and took his hand. I held it while he fell back asleep.

"I'm so sorry, Jess," I said the next day.

"About what?" His eyes were a little brighter, thank God. Not back to normal, but brighter.

"I'm sorry I made you do this. This treatment."

"Don't be sorry. Maybe it'll work." His voice was soft.

"But you—you don't think it will." I nearly choked on the words.

He looked away from me, at the wall. His answer was a whisper. "No."

"You never did, did you?"

He turned back and looked me in the eye. In a stronger voice, he said, "No."

"Why'd you do it, then?"

"For you." He reached for me and I took his hand. "Because you wanted me to fight."

"But you said you didn't want to die—"

"I don't, but I'm going to. I know it, Sam. Don't ask me how, but I know it. And that's okay—I accept it. But I'm also grateful for each moment I have, and I want to enjoy them. If I keep doing these treatments and buy a little more time . . . is it *worth* it to live in this stifling hospital room?"

He went on: "Someone posted a description of life on the cancer support website that I really like. They compared life to a stained-glass window, with each colored pane being a different part. Our health is only one piece—one we usually ignore. But when we get sick, it clouds up and we can't see through it; we stare at it, as if it's the only pane there is, and we ignore the beauty of all the other parts. But I want to look through the whole window, Sam, and I can't do that here."

I wasn't crying, but I was damn close.

"Don't be sad, Sam. We're all going to die, we can't escape it. I was miserable, I was feeling sorry for myself, but you changed all that. Your love touched me, and it was the beginning of my road back."

I clenched his hand and didn't say anything.

"Don't feel bad about what you did or didn't do. Please don't. What will that do, besides take away time from us?"

He was right. Guilt was a useless emotion, and it had been pretty darn destructive as well.

I squeezed his hand and promised not to waste any more time feeling bad. Or at least, try not to. But the way he was talking bothered me.

"You're acting like it's a done deal," I said. "Like you're already in the past tense."

"I don't mean to. Look, I'm getting the stem cell transplant. Who knows . . . maybe the treatment will work. But whether it does or it doesn't, when I leave here, I don't want to come back—ever."

I took in a deep breath, then let it out. "I understand."

Mom and I were sitting with Jess when the door to his room swung open and Gwen strode in, click-clacking in her heels.

"Well, well, the gang's all here," she said, I suppose in greeting.

"Hello, Gwen," Mom said. She was the only one who responded; I wouldn't speak to her unless I had to, and Jess wasn't speaking to her at all.

Gwen nodded at Mom. "Ellen." She came closer to the bed. "Jesse, how are you feeling today?"

Jess stared at the TV hanging overhead, just as if it were turned on.

"Still not talking to me?"

He hadn't said a word to her since the dinner. He was so pissed, he hadn't even brought his kitty pillow with him to the hospital.

"Jesse, may I please speak to you alone?"

After a few beats of silence, she turned to me. "Well, Samantha, if my son won't hear me out, will you?"

"Uh. . . . yeah, Gwen," I said. "Sure."

Jess grabbed my hand tight.

She said, "I heard you and Jesse the other night—I heard him tell you he wanted to end his treatments. I didn't mean to eavesdrop; I was about to knock, but, well, I had this feeling that something powerful was going on in there, between you two. So I listened at the door. I'm sorry."

She waited then, I guess to see if I would respond about that. But I was beyond caring about who heard what; and anyway, I'd done my share of eavesdropping myself.

Jess sat silently, squeezing my hand harder.

"What Jesse said to you—that hurt you, didn't it." It was a statement rather than a question, but I nodded anyway. She continued, "That was such a selfless thing you did—to support his decision. I—I don't think I could've done that."

She waited again, but still I said nothing.

"I saw then . . . how much you care about Jesse," Gwen said. "And then I realized that you don't want to take anything away from me; you just want to give him something back."

"Yes," I said, struck with a sudden affinity. "Yes—that's it, exactly."

Jess's grip lightened.

"I've thought about this a lot since then," Gwen said. "You love my son."

I nodded again.

"Then—then he has my permission to marry you."

Jess's hand loosened fully now, resting on mine without grabbing at all. "Mom?"

"Yes, Jesse?"

He reached his other hand out to Gwen. "Thanks, Mom."

She took it. "You're welcome, Jesse."

Chapter 27

Jess had his stem cell transplant.

They injected the cells right into the tube in his chest. He had to stay in the hospital another two weeks, until his bone marrow healed. A few days after the transplant, he started getting stronger—a little stronger every day. By the time he checked out of the hospital, he was taking baby steps around the room on his own. So far, so good. But the doctors could do nothing more but wait and see if the treatment had worked—if the cancer would stop spreading.

Five days after Jess got home, he was up and around again. We headed downtown to the city clerk's office on Worth Street with Mom and Gwen to get our marriage license. The following Sunday we were married by a judge in Central Park—in our spot.

Mom, Gwen, Maria, and Teddy were all there. So was Pete. He'd visited Jess a bunch of times in the hospital, and had hung out with us at home, too—the three of us. I'd told them how left out I'd felt; Pete certainly understood, after Jess had cut him out of his life, and they agreed that gender was irrelevant in friendship.

It was a perfect September day. The weather wasn't hot anymore, but it hadn't gotten too breezy, either. It felt like we were finally getting our place in the sun. The air was tinged with the scent of fall foliage and the aroma of warm, doughy pretzels.

I wore Mom's wedding gown, of simple white silk. Around my neck was a gold locket, a gift from Jess; there was a picture of him inside. Jess wore a black tux with a burgundy bow tie and cummerbund to match my bouquet. He looked incredible.

We'd each written our own vows. I went first:

"Jess, when I moved next door to you fourteen years ago, we felt an instant bond. You were my best friend growing up, and you still are. We played together, then loved together. And while we could say that we've been shadowed by sorrow, I'd rather say that we're surrounded by love, and that makes us the luckiest people on earth. I love you, Jess, now and forever, and I choose you as my husband."

Then it was Jesse's turn:

"Sam, I've always been a few steps behind you. It took the worst thing imaginable happening to me to realize the love we had. I'm so grateful for your companionship, your support, and most of all, for your heart. Today we stand here, where we spent so many hours of our lives together, in our oasis, our own field of dreams. It's a dream realized to be here, holding your hand. I love you, Sam, now and forever, and I choose you as my wife."

Teddy, wearing a miniature version of Jess's tux, jogged up and presented our rings. We slipped them on each other's fingers, both of us promising, "With this ring I pledge my love."

The judge said, "By the authority vested in me by the State of New York, witnessed by your friends and family, I have the pleasure to pronounce you husband and wife. You may now seal your vows with a kiss."

Everyone clapped when we kissed.

We went to celebrate at The View, a restaurant on the forty-sixth floor of the Marriott Marquis in midtown. The tables were on a slowly revolving circle, so that you got a 360-degree view of Manhattan while you ate. Watching the city from that high perch, I felt like I was sitting on top of the world.

We'd done it. We were married.

Everyone was happy and laughing together. It was a moment for the history books.

Gwen came from behind and hugged me. I whiffed her breath—she didn't seem drunk. "Samantha, I hope you'll join me in putting the past behind us."

"Sure, Gwen."

"If I must have a daughter-in-law, I'm truly glad it's you."

"Thanks." *Is that a compliment?*

Jess was watching us. Then he put his arm around her shoulder and pulled her into a hug. The day was a big hug-fest, which was definitely a good thing.

Jess went off somewhere, saying he'd be right back. Gwen sat back down by Mom, then Pete came over and gave me a kiss on the cheek.

"Hey, Mrs. Parker," he said, his eyes grinning widely. "I told you not to worry about Miss Pink."

Pete was barely recognizable without a baseball cap propped on his head. He wore a deep purple suit with threads of blue and yellow running through it. In the park he'd had an uncomfortable, squirmy kind of look on his face, and he'd tugged at his collar incessantly. I was surprised his tie was still on now; it was loosened, with the top shirt button undone—but still there. He looked relaxed, like he'd grown into his new skin.

"Thanks, Pete," I replied. "You're a good friend."

"Anytime, Sam."

I sat back down and Teddy bounced over, then plopped onto my lap.

"Sam, is Jesse my relative now?"

"Yeah, he's your brother-in-law."

"Then, would you care . . . "

"What, Ted?"

"We're having special relative day in kindergarten. Is it okay if I bring Jesse instead of you?"

I smiled. "Sure, Ted. I don't mind at all."

"Thanks, Sam. I'll catch ya next time." He hopped off my lap and jumped to the window on the tips of his toes to watch the world go 'round some more.

Jess came back and kissed me. "Did I tell you I love you today?"

"I think you mentioned it," I told him.

Just then a bunch of waiters came out. One was carrying a cake with two candles burning. They were singing: "Happy wedding to you, happy wedding to you, happy wedding day Sam, and by the way Jesse loves you."

"Just in case I forgot to mention it," Jess said.

The cake said: "I love you, Sam."

"Some things can never be overstated," he said. His eyes beamed with the reflection of the candles. "C'mon, let's both make a wish at the same time."

We puffed out those candles and everyone applauded. Then Mom clinked on a glass and said she had a toast:

"To Jesse and Samantha: You came up against life's cruelty and pain far too early, but by loving each other you found strength, comfort, and even triumph. Both of you sacrificed a part of yourselves for the other. That's a lesson to us all. I'm proud to be your mother and mother-in-law. Here's to you, kids!"

Everyone yelled "Cheers!" and sipped their drinks. Jess and I kissed.

"Hey, look at this!" Teddy shouted from his seat by the window.

Outside, a skywriter was hard at work. When he finished, the sky was filled with the fluffy white words:

"I love you Sam."

"Just in case I forgot to tell you," Jess said, wrapping his arms around me.

Chapter 28

October came.

The wind picked up. Spiky copper leaves fell from the trees, swirling in the wind. And my world crumbled down on top of me.

Jesse's cancer was spreading. The treatment hadn't worked.

Jess had been feeling okay since getting off his treatment. Just tired, that was all. I'd clutched a delicate feather of hope. . . .

Jess didn't get upset when Dr. Raab told him the news. He thanked the doctor for everything, and he even shook his hand. Dr. Raab asked if he was sure he didn't want to try anything else. Jess said he was sure.

I felt like I'd been hit by an eighteen-wheeler. Me and my feather, both plowed down, flat.

We left Dr. Raab's office and Jess linked his arm in mine, denim rubbing Windbreaker. Slowly, he led me back down the winding asphalt path dusted with leaves, through the bronzed park, back home.

He wanted to make love to me; that's all he asked for.

We'd been doing it pretty much constantly. He said he wanted to get in a whole lifetime's worth.

I slumped on the bed, lost in my despair.

Jess touched me. Raised hairs along my arm.

He caressed me, then whispered, "Focus on our love, Sam. It can't take that away from us." Then he touched me. . . .

When we finished, he lay in my arms. "This is how I want it to be," he said as I massaged the back of his neck.

"What?"

"When I get sicker. I don't want to go back to the hospital. Okay?"

"Okay." I still felt numb from the news, but the old tingling pain inched back into my veins. There was a familiar ache in my chest and I wondered, *How many times can a heart be broken?*

I'd told him I understood when he'd made the decision to end his treatment. And I did—I understood his reasons very well, and I respected them. I also hated them, but he didn't know that. *How can I tell him?*

He said, "I don't want a ton of painkillers, either. I know it's gonna be bad, and I don't care. I just want to be aware of every moment I have with you."

"Jesse . . . I heard the pain is unbearable—"

"They can give me something—maybe I can get the pump I read about in a pain control book, so I can regulate it myself. But I don't want to be zonked out. I want to have every second with you that I can. I'm telling you now, because I heard that sometimes you can't talk when . . . when it gets close."

I stroked his arm.

"Okay."

The pain in my heart intensified.

Fiery.

Scalding.

"I want you to hold me just like this—I want you to hold me when I die."

I ran my palm over the black fuzz on his head and kissed him. I had everything I could ever want, and soon I would have nothing.

"Okay," was all I said.

But it wasn't okay.

My husband was dying. How could that be okay?

It hurt so bad, but I couldn't talk to him about it. He'd found his peace, and of course I was glad. But I was at zero on the peace scale, and it was all I could do not to scream or cry at any given moment.

Dr. Chadwick did his best to help me.

We worked on the tapping at every session. I'd start on my wrist, tap three times, take three deep breaths in, out, in, out, in, out. Still tapping I'd say an affirmation: "I am loved and will never be alone." I'd repeat this on every spot covered in the tapping instruction book: the top of my head, my forehead, my cheeks, above my lip, my collar bone, the side of my left hand. As I spoke and tapped against my skin, I'd feel a tingling release . . . and for a moment I felt lighter. But the heaviness always came back, sometimes in minutes, sometimes in seconds. It was like a boulder on my chest.

"You're fighting it, Sam," Dr. Chadwick would say every time. "You're resisting your own recovery. Why do you think that is?"

I never answered him.

I didn't care why that was; I was tired of thinking. I was tired of trying to feel better.

All I wanted to do was curl up and be with Jess—not that it brought me any comfort. It felt like there was a time bomb ticking beside us, set to destroy. I'd wake up constantly, needing to feel him against me, needing to know he was there.

Due to my mental roadblocks the tapping was a bust, so Dr. Chadwick came on stronger about going to a support group. He'd been bringing it up for a while, but I'd ignored him. Who wanted to be in a roomful of misery? That was how I saw it.

I could see why Jess needed a group; that was different. Besides going online for support, he'd been heading downtown for meetings in Greenwich Village. Being with other people with cancer helped him so much, because they all understood.

But what—besides more sadness—was I going to get from meeting other people who'd lost or were about to lose someone they loved?

217

Then I came home one day and Jess told me I was looking pale and skeletal—like *I* was the one who was sick. I burst into tears, feeling guilty that I couldn't hide my despair from him, that I'd added my burden to his, even though I'd tried so hard not to.

He held me. And part of me felt so good in his arms, but another part wormed around so much, it felt like it would tunnel right out of my skin. After a while he said, "There's a group for caregivers that meets at the same time as my group."

I didn't say anything.

"Sam . . . please go to the meeting," he said softly.

I couldn't refuse my husband.

I was in a room filled with strangers.

It was a cozy room, I had to admit. Fluffy, cream-colored couches circled the perimeter of the room; a percolator gurgled coffee on a table in the corner, chocolate chip cookies were piled on a plate beside it. Lots of chatting people filled the room—women mostly, with a few scattered men thrown in. They were all older than me, some by a lot. It seemed like they all knew each other. Some of them were even laughing.

It was strange, seeing people in my situation laughing; I couldn't remember the last time I'd laughed, or even smiled.

Everyone was comfortable except for me.

All I really wanted to do was get through it, and get

back in a cab with Jess. Cuddled up next to him in the cab on the way there, I'd been able to pretend that we were going somewhere else, somewhere normal; that we were normal. But then we pulled up in front of the building and that was that—reality was back. We weren't normal.

And yet these people seemed able to function.

I sat there observing for a few more minutes, and then the meeting started.

"Welcome, everyone," the leader began. It was one of the men—a short, balding guy who looked to be around my mom's age. "I'm Tom. We'll open with the Serenity Prayer."

Did everything on earth revolve around the Serenity Prayer?

We all said it, and then the floor opened for discussion. It was an open night, meaning there was no set topic, and people talked about whatever was on their minds.

I just listened; I couldn't begin to open up like they were. It was way too much trouble to even think of where to start.

I felt like a foreigner; I'd assumed that everyone there would be consumed with their own problems, but they seemed able to cope and take care of themselves. The room wasn't filled with misery. Only I was distraught, which made me feel even more alone.

They called for a ten-minute break to get coffee. I got up and poured some, more to have an excuse to get up and do something than because I actually wanted it. Lately I didn't enjoy anything—nothing had flavor.

A thin woman with short blond hair who was probably in her thirties introduced herself to me as Sylvia.

"I'm Sam," I said.

"Your first time here?"

I nodded.

"I could tell. You have that look—the haunted look."

I didn't know what to say, so I said nothing.

"I didn't mean that in a bad way," she told me. "We all came in that way."

That was hard to imagine; she seemed so at ease. "Really?"

She nodded. "You'll feel better one day."

I looked at the wood floor, feeling guilty at even the thought of feeling better.

"It's not your duty to suffer, Sam," she said.

I looked back up at her, startled. It was like she'd read my thoughts.

"I've been there," she said. She touched my hand. Her compassion was almost too much to tolerate. "You didn't give your loved one cancer, Sam. You don't have to feel bad."

I held my breath and wished she'd let go.

"You don't have to suffer," she said.

I looked down again and shrugged.

"Just keep coming back," she said. "I promise you, it gets better."

Finally she released my hand.

I felt tingly, like when I did the tapping.

Maybe it was a good thing, being here, even if I couldn't participate. Maybe just being here was enough, for now.

"Okay," I told her. "I'll come back."

She smiled; it looked good on her. "Excellent," she said.

Jess and I didn't talk in the cab on the way home. Maybe he didn't want me to feel pressured to talk about the group, or maybe he was thinking about his own experience. It was just as well. I had a lot to process, and it would've been hard to say anything that made sense.

Silence was easy for us—we'd known each other so long.

I pressed into his arms, closed my eyes, and listened to the rhythmic groove of tires against the pavement. The shadowy city lights flickered across our faces, and we were warm and in motion. And for the first time in a long time, I felt just a little bit good.

Then I thought of Sylvia's smile.

I wondered what that would be like—to smile again.

Of course Mom was worried about me, too; there was no hiding anything from her. She was always asking me to come home for a meal, or at least a snack. So, the day after the support group meeting, I showed up at her door for breakfast.

Jess was still sleeping. It had been so tempting to just lay there with him, but something inside me had woken up at that meeting, and it wanted to get up and move.

Mom was so happy to see me. We sat at the kitchen table and she listed a smorgasbord of breakfast options. I told her I only wanted a toasted bagel with cream cheese. "Oh, fine," she said. "Be that way."

As the toaster oven hummed, I told Mom a little about the group. She was thrilled, of course. "I knew that was the right thing for you," she said.

The toaster dinged. She took out my bagel and smeared cream cheese over its nearly burnt top. Mmmm—just the way I liked it.

I crunched into the bagel; and for just a moment, I actually tasted it—it was delicious. But then guilt and sorrow flooded through me, and I felt so bad for having enjoyed that bite. What remained in my mouth suddenly tasted like cardboard. I dropped the rest of the bagel on my plate. It landed with a thud.

"Oh, Sam—," Mom said.

"Mom, don't." I couldn't take any more. The meeting had been enough.

"It's just—"

"I know what it is." She was going to say what Sylvia had said, but if I heard it again too soon—I just couldn't take that.

"Sam, it's not like I don't understand. Don't you think I miss your father? I talk to him all the time—"

"Do you ever see him?" The words came out before I could stop them.

"What?"

"I, uh— Oh, never mind," I said, stunned that I'd let my secret slip.

"Do *you* see your father?"

I couldn't lie to my mom. "Yeah, I do."

"Wow," she said. "Does he say anything to you?"

"No. It's always so quick. . . ." I told her about a few of the times I'd seen him. "I just thought maybe—you said you talked to him."

"I guess I'm not as lucky as you. I talk to the air and hope he hears me."

"Lucky? You think I'm lucky? It drives me nuts, seeing bits and pieces of him like that. Not having him whole . . . One night, I just smelled his cologne—and that was even worse."

"Maybe he's trying to tell you something."

"You don't think I'm crazy?"

"No, baby, not at all. There's so much evidence of life after death. . . . You're not alone in this, you know."

It was a relief, finally telling her—and having her believe me.

Teddy was at preschool; Mom suggested we go shopping.

And the funny thing was, I wanted to.

"You look better," Jess told me when I came back home.

"I told my mom—about seeing my dad," I said.

"And?"

"She took it well . . . didn't think I was bonkers at all."

"There you go, Sam. You have to learn to trust people. Have faith, you know?"

"Faith's a problem for me." As if he didn't know.

"Just take it one day at a time," he said.

And though it was a cliché, I knew he was right.

I went to bed thinking about Dad for the first time in ages. I mean, I thought about him a lot, but I always caught myself and stopped before I got in too deep—before I got to the memories that ached so much I thought I'd die if I let them surface.

Jess was already sleeping, breathing lightly, pressed tight against me like a warm shield. So I dropped my guard and did it: I remembered my dad.

A kaleidoscope of moments swirled through my mind. I remembered my dad holding me when I was little like Teddy and burning up with a fever, his cool lips kissing my forehead, his whisper that I was going to be fine.

I remembered my dad watching me in an elementary school play, cheering me loudly, even though I played the inauspicious, silent role—of grass.

I remembered my dad at the dinner table every night, always interested in the events of my day, even though each was remarkably similar to the one before it.

I remembered these and dozens of moments like them, so ordinary, and so unappreciated at the time. In and out they swelled, until I drifted off to sleep.

Then I heard a voice calling me back.

"Wake up, Sam."

"Jess?" I opened my eyes and asked, even though I knew it wasn't him. He was still asleep against me, still breathing in his light way. Easy breathing—something I doubted I'd ever experience again.

No, of course it wasn't Jess.

I knew who it was; I knew this voice so well. It was my dad.

But how could it be Dad? I must've been dreaming, but I felt awake. I even checked the clock: four a.m.

A long way from dawn, I'd conjured a ghost. Maybe I'd read too much Shakespeare.

"Look at me, Sam," my dead father said. I didn't want to; I squeezed my eyes shut and pushed my body against Jess like he was a barricade.

"Sam, it's time to look at me."

Time? When did spirits start worrying about time? What does time matter when you're dearly departed?

I didn't say this, or anything, out loud.

"All these months you've been thinking about me, calling me back with your thoughts, but then refusing to see what was right in front of you—refusing to look me in the face."

Was that why I'd never seen his face? All along I'd thought it was—that he wouldn't show himself fully. I couldn't understand why.

"That's right, Sam. You wouldn't look at me—"

"Stop it!" I broke in, eyes still shut. "Now you're reading my mind? That's awful! Don't I get any control in this, any privacy at all?"

"You're controlling everything, Sam. You're letting me into your mind. But part of you can't admit it to yourself."

There was a warmth in the room, like a fireplace was lit. The air carried his cologne.

He said, "Tell me what it is that's so painful."

But I couldn't. "You know, you have to know."

"You have to say it out loud. Let it out, honey. Let it out before it eats your insides."

I opened my eyes.

He was next to me, wearing the same blue suit he'd worn the last day of his life.

I stared at his tie, the light blue one with red polka dots that I'd adjusted for him because Mom had been busy with Teddy.

I couldn't look up.

He had no right to be here, so real, too real. He had no right to appear back in my life when all he was going to do was vanish again.

So I said it: "You left me."

There was a long pause.

Then he said, "Sweetheart, please look at me."

It had always been such a problem for me to look anyone in the eyes. I was afraid of seeing the truth in them, and maybe I was afraid of seeing myself.

But he was right. It was time. So I did it.

Finally, I looked him in the eyes.

Oh God, it hurt so bad. It hurt so bad to see how badly he was hurting.

"I'm sorry," he said. "I didn't *want* to leave you."

Of course he didn't want to—I knew that. But that was the logical part of me. The emotional part, that was a different story.

"Sam, the hurtful things in the world weren't designed to hurt you. They just are. Stop holding this grudge against the universe. You have to let go."

"Surrender," I said. It was maddening, how that kept coming up.

"Yes," he agreed. "Surrender your anger. Sam, when people are angry, all the wonders and the beauty of everyday life pass them by. All they have left is their rage. Is that what you want to happen?"

"I don't know how to let go," I said.

"You do, Sam. Live in the beauty of each moment."

"What's beautiful about this moment?" I demanded. "You're only going to leave me again, if you're even here at all. I've probably just gone mad!"

"You're not in the moment; you're worried about what comes next."

"Pardon me for not being perfectly Zen. Yes, I care about being left again!"

"Everyone leaves, Sam, in one way or another. But death can never rob us of the love we give away. Love stays with us—it never dies. You carry my love with you. Let go and feel it, Sam. Death is only an end if you see it as one."

"How can you say that? Of course it's an end," I said. I put my palm against Jess's back. "See how I can touch him, feel his warmth? I can't do that with you. You can't touch love, Dad."

He said, "Sam, that's the point. Death is an end to something limited—something physical. But it's not an end to love. Think about it, Sam. I know you're ready."

I grabbed on to Jess and squeezed into his arms. It was lucky he didn't wake up. Maybe part of me wanted him to wake up, to tell me if this was real. But he didn't.

"How do you know I'm ready?" I asked. He looked at me with so much love, it was almost like I *could* touch it.

"Because you called to me. You were ready to see."

Then he was gone.

Just like that—gone.

I thought I'd cry. But I didn't; there was nothing left. No tears, and maybe no reason to cry.

I felt hollow, kind of spent. But I also felt on the cusp of something. For the first time in a long time, I felt like there was a way out. I wasn't there yet, but reaching it was a possibility.

My dad's words floated through my mind: "Death can never rob us of the love we give away."

I closed my eyes and drifted to sleep.

me and jesse
in the park
on the
blanket
with
red and white
squares
pretzel smell

The Girl Next Door

in
the
air
jesse
leans on me
he is
warm
we are
tired
we
bang heads
laugh
laugh
his
curly black hair
tickles
my
cheek
we
played
tag
zig-zagged
round and
round one
two
three
trees
three like me
i won
he said

i
did
not
win
i fell
yuck grassy mouth
grassy nose tickles
laugh
laugh
he fell
too
on me
we
banged heads
laugh
laugh
he smells like
bubble
gum
he says i
won
i was
ahead
but
i fell
on accident
he
did not
wind blows
gentle

pretzel smell
in
the
air
jesse leans
warm
warm
warm on me
voice
across the squares
mom
turns
pages
story time

I woke up the next morning remembering my dream, remembering the love Jesse and I gave away that day to each other.

"Morning, Sam." Jess smiled at me. That love was still there, all these years later. Dad was right—it wouldn't die.

"Morning, Jess." I smiled back.

In that moment I felt peace.

That's what letting go was.

It was as simple as a smile.

Chapter 29

December was mild, for December. We wore coats, but hats and gloves weren't necessary.

December was harsh, for Jess. He weakened, started to fade.

His body hurt him, but he wasn't sore emotionally.

He thanked me for my love.

He said all he wanted was for me to be with him.

Now, I could be there for him.

And we'd had a great November.

I helped Jess slip his coat on and wheeled him out of the apartment. We were going into the park to celebrate my birthday. It was December 11, and I was eighteen.

"Happy birthday, Sam," he told me in his weak, almost whispering voice when we got to our spot. I bent to be level with him and we kissed. He handed me the thin, rectangular box he'd been holding.

I tore into the crinkly silver wrap. It was the poem he'd written for me, framed. I stared at it, then burst into tears, something I hadn't done in a long time.

"Hey, I didn't mean to make you cry," he said.

"I'm sorry, Jess . . . It's just—so beautiful." I wiped my face with my sleeve, heaved a breath in and out, and looked him in the eye. "I have to confess; I read your poems."

"Did you?" He wasn't bothered at all, just surprised. "What'd you think of them?"

"I guess— I guess I thought they were incredibly sad."

"Yeah. That's why I didn't show them to you." He spoke slowly, with effort. "They were . . . they were like therapy for me, but I didn't want to upset you."

He'd been trying to spare me, like I'd been trying to spare him.

"God, I love you so much," I said. I kissed him.

"Your other present is back home, but I wanted to tell you about it here. Because it really couldn't be wrapped. . . ." He stopped and coughed.

"You okay, Jess?"

He nodded. "Anyway, I got you—us—a star. I bought a star and named it 'Sam & Jess's Place in the Heavens.' " He coughed again. "The certificate's wrapped up at home. I just wanted . . . I wanted to tell you here. I got the idea on prom night, when we were staring at the stars, dancing under them."

"Aww, Jess." I hugged him, and couldn't say anything else.

He ran his fingers through my hair. "After I'm gone . . . talk to our star. I'll be listening."

We sat there in silence then, in our place. We didn't have to speak to communicate, to relive all our times there. To see the grass stains on our knees, hear our laughter as we chased each other round and round the trees, smell the pretzels in the air, feel the sun shine on our cheeks.

We had a place just for us.

That was more than a lot of people had.

I knew then that it was true—that the love we'd given each other would stay there always, indestructible. I absolutely felt it in the air, and in my heart.

I walked up the path to a stand and bought us two hot chocolates.

We sipped, steam piping up our noses. Still we sat, remembering. The warmth of the drink spread through my body and settled in my bones.

It was then that I felt the second half arrive—the remaining part of the relief I'd felt when Jess had proposed. I hadn't expected it, and I didn't know I'd been missing it, but there it was.

It felt permanent, this peace.

It felt real.

It felt right.

After a while, Jess spoke. He asked if I remembered the talk we'd had about his ashes. *Of course I do.* He said he'd been wrong, that he didn't want me to be burdened by keeping his ashes, and that he was afraid I wouldn't be able to move on, staring at a silver urn every day. Before I could say anything, he told me what he wanted instead.

He wanted to stay in our place, always. He wanted me to plant a tree for him, and scatter his ashes in its soil. He wanted me to come sit with him under our star.

He said to visit him, but not exclusively.

He urged me to go on, for us both.

He asked me not to give up on my life.

I agreed.

Chapter 30

We've been in bed, listening to Abba on low. Jess is against me on his side, lying on my arm. He's shaking, but he's yanked the tube that was attaching the pump with painkillers to his vein, and he turns away from the morphine lollipop I hold toward him.

I blink away tears and face the bedside table, trying to absorb everything about this moment. I scan the opening of my poem, propped next to the clock.

Eternity, evermore

That's how long your love is for

The red numbers on the clock say twelve o'clock. It's midnight. Christmas Day.

I take a quick swipe at my eyes and turn around. "Happy birthday, Jess." I kiss his lips.

Jess is gripping the sheet—so hard that his knuckles are white and his veins are bulging. I offer him the lollipop again.

"Sweetheart, please . . ." I can't stand to watch him suffer anymore, can't bear to feel his constant quivering with pain.

I see it in his eyes and maybe he sees it in mine, because he finally nods and accepts the lollipop. It clicks around in his mouth, against his teeth.

Outside, the temperature's fallen. Fat flakes blur the night, swirling, surrounding, cloaking the pavement, entombing the city. I stare at the shrouded trees across the street in Central Park. Weighted in white, distorted, they look both beautiful and frightening. I squint to see the winding path through the park. It's covered, nearly obliterated by numbing snow.

My eyes move from the window back to Jess. "I love you," I tell him, smoothing my fingers on his skin.

He nods.

I run my hand down Jess's trembling back, trying to make him feel better while the morphine kicks in. The music's over. The only sounds in the room are faint clangs and hisses from the heating system—that and Jess's labored breathing.

The snow is unrelenting.

The city is obscured.

Jess's head lies nuzzled in the crook of my neck. Our bodies are entangled, his heart hammering against me. I glide my pinky along his cheek, absorb his warmth.

I'll love you from the heavens
for eternity,

     Evermore.

Acknowledgments

Thanks to Evelyn M. Fazio for being a lovely editor and a lovely person.

Thanks to my teacher, Bunny Gabel, for helping me sort this novel out, and to my classmates for their thoughts and crucial support.

Thanks to The New School Graduate Writing Program for providing a "think tank" environment, and helping me take that terrifying leap to novelist (it was like bridging the chasm in *Star Wars*).

Thanks to the Long Island Society of Children's Book Writers and Illustrators for their early encouragement and continuous camaraderie, and to all my writing friends I've collected over the years (there are a lot of them!) for being the superb human beings they are. Special gratitude to Lynne Marie Pisano.

Thanks to Pascale Laforest for helping me with some specifics, and Susan Abrahams for providing a crucial plot point. Thanks to Cheryl Lazarus for leading me to Forrest Church's beautiful book, *Love & Death*.

Thanks to Caryn Wiseman for her valuable help, especially in sorting out Gwen.

Thanks to Carolyn P. Yoder for believing I could write a novel and convincing me of that (though the one she was referring to wound up being a picture book, and a fine one at that).

Thanks to my mom—Norina—and my Aunt Olga for encouraging and fostering my love of writing, and particularly for their patience in Arthur Treacher's Fish & Chips the day inspiration struck and I jotted copious story notes on a stack of yellow napkins when I was about nine. This was my first inkling that my writing was important and worth waiting for.

Thanks to Tony Castrovilla and Barbara Castrovilla for providing me the time and space I needed to write.

Thanks to God and the universe for each and every gorgeous moment, and for the incredible path I'm on.

Thanks to my precious sons, Michael and Casey, for putting up with my idiosyncrasies (there's a fine line between lunatic and novelist) and loving me unconditionally.

Thanks to the cancer survivors who generously shared their stories with me.   Thanks to Amy White at I'm Too Young For This! Cancer Foundation, Heidi Adams at Planet Cancer and Jonny Imerman at Imerman Angels for their gracious help.